DATE DUE

DEMCO 38-296

The
CANDY VENDOR'S
BOY
and Other Stories

Beatriz de la Garza

Houston, Texas
1994

K

upport from the National
gency), the Lila Wallace-
W. Mellow Foundation.

Arte Público Press
University of Houston
Houston, Texas 77204-2090

Cover design by Mark Piñón

De la Garza, Beatriz Eugenia.
    The candy vendor's boy / by Beatriz de la Garza.
        p.   cm.
    ISBN 1-55885-106-2 : $9.95
    I. Title.
PS3554.E1138C36 1994
813'.54—dc20   93-29313
                                                         CIP

Contents

To Nela,
with love and gratitude

The
CANDY VENDOR'S
BOY
and Other Stories

The
Candy Vendor's
Boy

He was coming home in a snowstorm. Danny thought this was somehow fitting, the weather being as momentous as the occasion. Looking out of the train window, he could see the snow being blown by the wind like sand and piled up in drifts against the barbed wire fences. He had seen snow before, but never this much. The newspaper had said this was the heaviest snowfall in Texas in the twentieth century. And he was coming home in the midst of it, coming home for the first time as a soldier.

It was already dark when the train pulled into Austin. Not many passengers got off. The news of stranded trains in snowbanks back East had kept the timid from traveling. But not Danny. This was his first leave in six months, his first chance to come home since he had signed up last summer, soon after the war had started. It was still snowing, but the snow was now much lighter and softer. Large, luxuriant snowflakes drifted leisurely through the air. It was not yet eight o'clock, but the streets were deserted, the storefronts dark, and only the streetlights glimmered at long intervals. Danny's footsteps made no sound in the deserted street and, for a moment, he wondered if he was in the middle of a dream.

As he approached the shanties by the river, though, he knew he was awake. He could smell the smoke from their chimneys, even the faint stench from the city dump by the river, where putrefaction had been delayed by the cold. In the summer, when the breeze was from the south, the smell would be unbearable, but now it could almost pass unnoticed.

The house, a frame shack on stilts, clung precariously to

the creek embankment off Ruiz Street. It lay a hundred yards or so upstream from where the creek emptied into the river and had been one of the few structures that had escaped the terrible flood three years before. He climbed the worn stone steps that were embedded into the creek bank and that led to the sagging front porch. Here smoke was pouring out of the chimney too. Before knocking, he paused for a minute to look inside through the front window, the only one with glass.

A lighted kerosene lamp rested on the kitchen table, flickering fitfully, and showed several figures sitting immobile around the table. He had no sooner knocked on the door than it flew open, and his little sister, Lupita, stood in front of him, beaming. He hugged and kissed her, and then the others, who just a minute before had sat not moving, now milled about him, all talking at the same time.

There was his older sister, Hermelinda, thin and pale, looking older than her twenty-five years. His mother, wiping her hands on her apron and smoothing back her gray hair, came forward to hold him with a strength not to be expected from her slight frame. His older brother, Norberto, was there too, tall and bullnecked, his arm and shoulder muscles grown formidable from carrying beef carcasses on his back. His quiet wife, obviously pregnant, and their two young children stood behind him. And there was his father, getting up laboriously from his chair by the fire. Danny had been told that his father had once been like Norberto, tall and strong. He had been a blacksmith, but a horse had kicked him and then fallen on him, almost killing him. He had kept his head away from the horse's hoofs, but his back was broken. He managed to leave the sickbed eventually, but he had become a hunchback.

Danny bent down and put his arms around the gnarled figure of the old man, his lips brushing his father's forehead. He had never seen his father cry, but now the old man stood looking at him with unusually bright eyes. As if to hide the emotion, he reached out and touched the sleeve of Danny's overcoat. "Very nice fabric," he said, "very good wool." Suddenly Danny became conscious of his heavy overcoat, the wool uniform underneath and the new boots on his feet. He took off his coat and threw it over a chair.

That night they had Christmas and New Year's celebration in mid-January. The family had held off on all festivities until he came home, Lupita said, as his mother removed a steaming tin can full of tamales from the fireplace. His mother, to whom sitting idle was unnatural, then began to fry the New Year's pastries, the *buñuelos*, in a heavy skillet. Danny reached in his pocket and pulled out a small roll of dollar bills—twenty—saved from his pay of six months. It was enough for more than a month's rent, and he gave them to his father, who took them without looking at him.

Without being told, Danny knew what the unusually cold weather had done to his father's work. Lupita, however, felt no reticence and was telling him as she hung from his arm, "Yesterday Papá fell on the ice when he was trying to go out with the candy, and today he couldn't go out at all either because it was snowing so hard. Mamá told him it was no use going out because nobody would be out in the street to buy candy or tamales, but I saw many children playing in the snow. I wanted to play too, but Mamá wouldn't let me because I would catch cold."

Lupita went on chattering and stopped only when the *buñuelos* came out of the skillet, crisp and sizzling. Lupita sprinkled them with sugar and ground cinnamon. As they ate, Danny looked around him, happy that they were all together. No, not all together, he told himself. His happiness clouded at the thought of Magdalena, his sister who was two years older than him and who had left them four years earlier. A regular customer of The Golden Door saloon, which was half a block away from the house, had seduced her when she was fifteen. After this had been discovered, it turned out that the man was married and that he had left town. So did Magdalena, whether with him or alone, or with someone else, no one ever knew. Magdalena was never mentioned again, but Danny still thought about her at times like these.

Danny told them about army life in Camp Bowie, about Fort Worth, where none of them had ever been, about the

141st Infantry Regiment to which he belonged. There were only a handful of Mexicans in the 141st, he told them, although many of his fellow soldiers didn't even know he was Mexican. They should hear what they called him. Nobody could say "Aramberri"; they had never heard the name before, so they called him "Berry." He explained what "Berry" meant in Spanish, and they all nodded and smiled politely. His friends called him "Danny," just like Doctor Baines always had, and he liked that.

He told them next of his good fortune: he was a truck driver in the Army. Could they imagine that? He had been told when he signed up that he would probably be a cook. Instead, they had taught him to drive a truck and to repair it. When they went to France—here he paused to let everyone absorb the immensity of what he was saying—he would drive supply trucks to the front line. His mother crossed herself at the sound of these words, and he felt sorry that he had said anything about the war. His mother felt only fear at the mention of it. She had no thoughts for glory or the excitement of traveling and seeing the world outside, as he had.

Norberto was clearing his throat now, getting ready to speak. He spoke with a slight stutter, so it always cost him great effort to say anything. Danny looked at him affectionately, this giant of a brother who had been his protector in the days when Danny was a spindly-legged, pale and sickly child.

"Do you think they will take me, too?" Norberto's words rushed out together in his effort to not stumble over them. He paused, and the family knew better than to prod him; it would only make the pause longer. "I am not afraid to fight," he finally added. Danny thought it was almost comical that Norberto should say that. Not many men had wanted to fight Norberto. "But, if I go," he continued after another pause, "what will happen to these ones?" He cocked his head in the direction of the two children who clung to their mother's legs.

"You don't have to worry, Beto. They make exceptions for men like you, with a family to support. Have you told them that? What did you do with those papers you got?"

Norberto shook his head, his face turning red. Danny had

not been there to deal with the papers; Danny was the only one who could read and write. "I threw them away."

"I will look for Doctor Baines tomorrow. He can help you when I'm not here. He understands enough Spanish for you to be able to talk to him. All you have to do is ask him."

When Danny was a young boy and had just learned the rudiments of catechism, he had tried imagining what God looked like. He could not decide whether God looked like the priest or like Doctor Baines. He had settled on Doctor Baines because he had a gray beard.

Danny remembered lying in a cot as a child, his bones aching and his face burning, and Doctor Baines coming in often, his hands smooth and cool and smelling of soap as they touched his forehead. Sometimes he would leave behind bitter-tasting medicine, sometimes candy, saying that just because Danny's father made candy, it didn't mean Danny got to eat it. And it was true; Danny hardly ever had candy, didn't even like it. Waking up in the morning to the cloying smell of caramelized sugar and watching his father stirring in the goat's milk into the sugar as the kettle stood on the fire, Danny's stomach would contract, and he would refuse all food. Doctor Baines' candy was different though, lemon or peppermint flavored. He enjoyed that.

It was Doctor Baines, too, who had took Danny to the school when he got well; he told the teacher that she must teach the boy to read and write. The teacher had been too much in awe of Doctor Baines to protest that Mexican children did not come to her school.

Danny did indeed learn to read and write and do arithmetic. He stayed in school until he was twelve, and his father's pride in him and in his accomplishments was clear for all to see. When his mother and his older sisters washed and ironed the linen from the university houses, they washed and ironed his clothes, too, with as much care as if they belonged to a professor's child. After he regained his strength and began to grow too big for his clothes, his poor, timid mother, unable to make herself speak, had Magdalena ask the professors' ladies if they had old children's clothing to give away. The individual garments thus acquired sometimes looked odd when combined, and they did not always fit, but they were always washed and ironed.

Danny's father, who had learned to read in Spanish from his own father a long time before but had subsequently forgotten, began asking Danny to read to him. When he took Danny with him to the Avenue to help him sell candy, he would sometimes pick up a newspaper that someone had discarded on the sidewalk and ask his son to tell him what it said. Danny became quite a proficient translator in this manner. And Norberto was always there to fight his fights with the bigger neighborhood boys who called him a sissy because he went to school every day with his slate under his arm.

After Danny turned twelve and finished the sixth grade, he had to leave school. Norberto had gotten married and had to support a wife, and his father was suffering from such a bad relapse of back pain he could barely move. Danny went to work helping to deliver bread and milk. He had worked before; after all, he had helped his father sell candy, but now work was his complete world outside the house—the delivery wagons in the daytime and the three-room shanty at night.

Gone was the schoolhouse where he could observe the classmates that hardly spoke to him. Their very silence and indifference, though, had made it possible for him to be free to imagine any kind of life for them. And through them he could dream of the kinds of houses they lived in, the families they had, the clothes they wore, the foods they ate. Later, making the rounds in the wagon, he got to see some of those houses—the kitchens facing the alleys, mostly—and he even occasionally recognized some of his former schoolmates or their parents. But he tried not to dwell on that. Seeing them was usually a disappointment; he had given them better lives in his imagination.

He left the delivery wagon for the bakery itself after two years. He became a baker's apprentice and for more than three years inhaled the flour dust that floated in the air and covered everything, including him, while he stoked the fire and checked the ovens. Even in cold weather the bakers would strip to their undershirts as they worked in those stuffy rooms. Danny felt sometimes that he would faint if he did not get fresh air. Then, when the United States entered the war, Danny began to think that there was, perhaps, a way out of the bakery and even out of the shanty by the river. He signed up as soon as he was of age and left Austin. Six months later, he was back for a visit, feeling that he was a different person.

The morning after his return, he was up at daybreak and out of the house, stopping only to drink a mug of coffee that his mother had pressed on him. The steps were icy, and he slid on the bottom two, but he did not stop. He wanted to be outside and breathe the cold, crisp air of morning. The closeness of those three rooms upstairs with their smell of cooking and ashes from the fireplace seemed to paralyze his lungs.

He stood motionless for a few moments, inhaling deeply and feeling the cold air burn his throat and chest. He looked around at what once had been a familiar landscape but was now transformed under a white blanket into unrecognizable shapes. The sky had cleared during the night and was now a dazzling blue. From where he stood he could see how the swiftly running creek emptied into the river, and as he looked, the sun, coming over the horizon, touched the surface of the water and broke it into countless slivers of light.

He retraced his steps of the night before, noticing as he did, how the indentations of his footprints were still in the snow. He climbed out to the street where the creekbed was shallow; soon he was walking east, towards the Avenue and past The Golden Door. Its proprietor, a man of foreign origin with a fierce-looking moustache and sorrowful eyes, was sweeping the snow that had collected on the front porch. He did not recognize Danny at first in his soldier's uniform, but when he did, he wished him a happy and prosperous 1918 and was profuse in his praise of young men who served their country. He asked Danny to drop in for a drink later on—on the house, he clarified. It might be Danny's last drink, he added lugubriously, but then hastened to explain in embarrassment that he did not foresee any evil for Danny. It looked as if the Prohibitionists were going to have their way, and nobody would be drinking anything stronger than lemonade. He would like to see an army that drank nothing but lemonade. Danny thanked him and promised to return later that evening to claim his drink.

Nobody was stirring in the house next to The Golden Door. There was no sign here to advertise the house business, but it was not necessary. Almost anyone who was interested knew it was a brothel. Five or six girls usually resided there with the madam, but they were all late risers. Danny remembered seeing the women since he was a child—not the same ones, of course, for they came and went at intervals. He had always been a little in awe of them. They appeared to him as remote idols of a secret cult into which he had not been initiated. One day, he looked up as he walked by and saw one of them in her underwear in front of a second-story window. From then on he always looked up at that window when he passed by, but the apparition did not occur again.

When Danny was sixteen, three years after Magdalena had run away, he began meeting one of the girls from the brothel—Dora—on Sunday afternoons, when most of the other girls were out. He knew who she was even before she spoke to him. He knew, for example, that Dora was one of the most sought-after girls in the house, although she was not particularly pretty. She had long, thick black hair and large, dark eyes set in a pale, thin face. Danny decided that what made her attractive was the contrast between those somber eyes, surrounded by bluish circles and a full, perfectly shaped mouth that never smiled. Or perhaps it was the unexpectedly large breasts on such a thin body. At any rate, there was an element of surprise in Dora, although she, herself, seldom seemed moved by anything.

That first Sunday he looked up to the second story windows, as he usually did, and saw someone there again, not in her underwear, but wrapped in a loose kimono. His footsteps slowed down and came to a stop under her unwavering gaze. Dora finally motioned with her head that he should come up and pointed to the back door. She met him at the foot of the service stairs and led him up, holding her finger to her lips to forestall any talk. The house was completely silent, except for some loud snores that came from behind a door on the first floor and the shrill, whirring sound of the cicadas in the afternoon heat outside.

Dora led him to her room and, once in it, to her bed, which was still unmade. She began to undress him, her fingers lightly touching him on the neck, the shoulders, over his body. She was about to introduce him to the mysteries of sexual intercourse, but he could not wait. She assured him that the next time he would be more patient, and she began to dress him again. He started to tell her that he thought he wanted to try then, but she shook her head and said no; the madam was sleeping downstairs and would wake up soon because she had to go out calling at five. She told him to come back the following Sunday afternoon before three.

Danny then remembered that, for Dora at least, the encounter was a matter of business, and he told her that he would have money the following week. She shook her head dismissing the subject. It would be free for him, but the madam mustn't find out. He was a beautiful young man, she said, touching his cheek and then his eyes. "Such long eyelashes," he heard her murmur.

Danny was back the following Sunday and almost every Sunday for the next six months or so. He developed patience and proficiency with practice. Then he missed her at the window one cold Sunday in February. At the end of the week, he had finally asked at The Golden Door, and one of the customers had laughed knowingly at him. "Why do you want to know? You couldn't afford Dora. She always had a soft spot for pretty looking youngsters like you, though. Took them on as guests—non-paying guests." He laughed enormously at his joke, and Danny felt his face turning red. "She's gone," the man said. "Back to wherever she came from. Took sick or something, or maybe the madam kicked her out for giving away free samples." And that was all that Danny could find out about Dora.

He tried remembering where Dora said she was from.

She had never talked much about herself, although Danny had asked her. Once she mentioned something about her mother being Cuban, and alluded vaguely to New Orleans, all frustratingly imprecise. Danny always found himself wanting to know people's histories, but Dora had defeated him.

So had his own mother; she could tell him little beyond her parents' names. From his father, Danny at least had a history that went back to another generation and another country.

Danny's grandfather, his father's father, was born in Mexico, had fought against the French and had to escape across the border—all this his father had told Danny. Among his father's family there was at least one prominent Aramberri soldier-patriot who led the fight against the invaders. Danny's grandfather, however, had not remained in Mexico long enough to become a hero. When he got tired of fighting, he crossed the river and the border and then started to fight all over again—to make a living this time. He made his way to Central Texas, working on the railroads and doing odd chores for ranchers eventually marrying a local woman with whom he had several children. Except for Danny's father, little was known of the others now. It was from his grandfather, according to Danny's father, that Danny inherited the strange-hued gray eyes and pale, translucent skin that had fascinated Dora.

Dora had faded gradually from Danny's memory, having little to remember her by except for those Sunday afternoons. He never told anyone about them, never wanting to boast about the affair or share its details with others. Perhaps it was the contrast between the clothes drying in the sun behind his own house and the dampness of the sheets in Dora's shadowy bedroom made him feel relief at not having to lie anymore in Dora's unmade bed that smelled of rumpled linen.

He made his way to the Avenue. A few shopkeepers were unlocking their doors and opening shutters, but there were few people about. The snow had hardened to ice in patches and made walking hazardous. He slipped two or three times, but caught himself before falling. Once he clutched at a lamp post to keep his footing and caught a reflection of himself in a shop window. He began to laugh, partly at his comical predicament, but mainly because he felt happy. He was young, eighteen years old, he felt healthy and strong, and he knew he looked handsome in his uniform.

He walked up the Avenue to the Capitol grounds where he found children engaged in snowball fights and sledding down the hills on washboards. He helped them make snowballs and pushed their makeshift sleds. By midmorning, he had returned to the Avenue, ambling slowly and looking in the shop windows. The Red Cross had opened a canteen next door to the Bon Ton café. A sign in the window welcomed servicemen and promised hot cocoa inside. He tried the door without much hope and was surprised to find it unlocked.

He walked in and found a middle-aged lady hanging up her coat. He started to make his excuses and leave, but she insisted that he stay and assured him that she would make cocoa in no time at all. He looked at the posters that lined the wall while she busied herself with a small kerosene stove. She finally put a steaming mug of cocoa in front of him. While he drank, he answered her questions as to where he was stationed. She was proud that he was a hometown boy, and told him that the newspaper had been running stories on local boys in the armed services. Perhaps they would also write about him. She was about to embark on questions about his family, when another woman joined her, and, while the two commented on the weather, he managed to thank them for the cocoa and make his escape.

He collided with a passerby as he stepped out of the canteen. Midway through the apologies, Danny realized that the other man was Nicolás Moreno, an old friend of Norberto's. Nico did not recognize Danny until Danny made himself known to him. Nico then threw his arms around him and began speaking Spanish to him. He wanted to know what Danny had been doing and praised his fine appearance and his patriotism.

"I am proud of you," Nico said, patting him on the arm.

"You were always a very smart boy. You will go far in the Army. But, what are you doing, wandering around in the cold?"

Danny shrugged his shoulders and said he just wanted to be outdoors.

"That's very well, but don't catch cold. You don't have to be out walking in the cold by yourself, anyway. You should let people show their gratitude to you for serving the country and enjoy yourself at the same time. Why don't you come to the tea dance this afternoon?"

Danny looked at the other man with surprise, and Nico pointed to a poster behind him, in the canteen window. He had not seen that one before. It advertised a *thé dansant* that afternoon, Saturday, from three to six at the Knights of Columbus Hall. Danny shook his head.

"Don't say no before you even know what it is. It's ladies—yes, American ladies—serving punch and pastries and dancing with the soldiers on leave. All very respectable and chaperoned and very elegant. I play in the orchestra—for the dancing. They needed another violin, since the regular one went into the Army. I have this bad leg, you know, so I can't go, and they needed someone, so I got the job. The only Mexican in the orchestra."

"They won't let me in a place like that," he stated, matter of factly.

"They let me in, don't they, to play for them? That's because they need me. And, of course, I also wear a suit, and I am clean. And I speak English, and my skin is light," he added as an afterthought. "You look very fine in your uniform," he continued. "You are a handsome young man. In these times of war, people don't look too closely behind the uniform if it's worn by a handsome young man. I want you to hear me play with this orchestra. It's a good orchestra. As a favor to me, will you come?"

Danny finally agreed to do so.

Later that day, Danny took a streetcar to the Knights of Columbus Hall and arrived there by three, but it was three-thirty before he forced himself to go in. It was the cold that did it. He had stood on the sidewalk, stamping his feet every now and then, watching other soldiers go in, some alone, some in small groups. Some ladies also arrived in an automobile and stepped gingerly on the icy sidewalk, their heavy coats with fur collars held closely around them as they ducked inside. He decided to go in only long enough to warm up and then leave.

Inside there was a small foyer that led into a large room which was brightly lit by a chandelier with electric candles. A large fire burned at the far end of the room, and the first impression he received as he walked in was of an overly bright and overheated room.

There were many more soldiers than ladies, and the latter were both young and old. The weather had obviously deterred all but the most hardy or the most duty-minded from attending. The orchestra was playing on a small, raised dais at one end of the room, and half a dozen couples were dancing to a waltz. A stout, gray haired matron offered him hot punch, and he was so flustered that all he could do was nod dumbly as she put a cup in his hand.

He stood alone in a corner, sipping nervously from his cup, the taste of cloves biting into his tongue and the roof of his mouth. He wondered if he would meet anyone who remembered him from school or, worse yet, from the bakery, but everyone around him was a stranger. The orchestra was breaking up for a rest now, and he saw his friend put down the violin and look around the room. Nico saw him, then, and came towards him.

"So you came, after all. I am glad." Nico clapped him on the shoulder and jostled the hand that held the cup. Danny nodded and, to avoid any accidents, quickly gulped down the remaining punch, cloves and all, his mouth and nostrils tingling as he did so.

"Why aren't you dancing? There are all those pretty ladies wanting to dance with a soldier."

Out of the corner of his eye Danny saw a redheaded girl in a bright blue dress offering cookies to other soldiers and wondered if the other people could overhear them. If they heard them speaking Spanish, would they tell them to leave?

Nico did not seem concerned, though; perhaps he didn't worry because he knew they needed him to play.

"I'm going to ask the orchestra director to let you play a number."

Danny was horrified. "No, don't do that," was all he could say.

"He's a good man, an Italian. You ought to see how many foreigners there are here now. He likes me—we get along. I'll tell him you were always a good player, that I taught you how to play."

And before Danny could say anything else, Nico was gone. While he looked around for a place to put down his cup so he could leave unobserved, Nico returned, smiling broadly.

"He says it will be an honor to have one of our brave soldiers play with his orchestra. 'Over the Waves'—you remember how we played it at all the weddings? That's what I told him you'll play."

One part of him told Danny to get out of that room immediately before he exposed himself to ridicule, while another part stood by and watched himself climb to the dais. He took the violin from Nico, tested the strings, essayed a few tentative bars, and took his place with the orchestra. The music engulfed him completely, and when he finally looked up from the violin at the couples dancing below, he saw at first the dark, perspiring faces, intent on the dance, of the Mexican weddings of summers ago. Then his eyes focused, and he saw the ladies in their rich winter frocks and the uniformed soldiers that glided sedately around the room.

"Over the Waves" was such a graceful waltz—one of his favorites—but he thought the dancers moved stiffly: the soldiers as if anxious to not appear to presume, the ladies conscious of the honor they were conferring. Many of the soldiers lined the walls around the room and stood talking among themselves, the glass punch cups looking ridiculously small in their hands, while their eyes followed the dancers.

He saw the redheaded girl dancing with a tall, thin corporal. She came up only to his shoulder, and he had to stoop to keep his arm around her waist, but she seemed oblivious to her partner's awkwardness. Her head was tilted back slightly, and her eyes were half-closed. Her lips were parted also, but that was probably because her front teeth were rather prominent, as Danny could see from observing her profile. They were almost directly below him, and he noted also her bright copper hair which was held at the top of her head with combs, except for a few tendrils that escaped at the back and curled at the nape. He thought her hair was beautiful.

The waltz ended, and the orchestra was taking a bow. The Italian conductor put his arm around Danny's shoulders and asked, "What is your name, private?" Danny told him, and the conductor repeated it with surprisingly good pronunciation. "We must thank this talented young man, one of our brave soldiers, Private Daniel Aramberri." Danny had said Dahniel and not "Daniell"; so had the conductor, and nobody seemed the wiser when they heard the surname. A hearty applause followed the introduction and continued as Danny stepped down from the platform. He felt a warm flush of happiness, and even triumph, go through him, and his face broke out in an unaccustomed smile.

The redheaded girl was standing alone in the middle of the dance floor, still applauding and looking at him and what could be interpreted as nothing but admiration. Still in the throes of his newly-found confidence, he heard himself asking her for the honor of the next dance, and she put her arms out to him. It was the "Blue Danube" this time, and Danny was glad of it. He was a good dancer, and waltzes were what he danced best. They were the best dancers in the room—Danny because the music flowed from inside him and animated his movements, the girl because she was happy to follow someone who knew what he was doing.

Only when the music stopped did Danny look at her. He was surprised at the bright blue of her eyes, the same hue as her dress. Electric blue, it was called, he recollected. Of course, that was why she wore that color. Those startling blue eyes and that copper hair were her glory. Otherwise, she was just a little thing with pale, freckled skin, a snub nose and the prominent teeth that gave her a breathless look.

She was not poor; the smooth touch of the wool flannel of her dress and the richness of the velvet trim on her collar and cuffs told him that. It was an amazing feat for Danny to have danced with her. He thanked her for the dance, and she gave him a brief little nod and moved away to pick up a platter from the refreshment table. He followed her progress around the room as she dutifully offered the plate of fruitcake and cookies to the soldiers standing stiffly about. She did not smile as she did so, and her eyes remained downcast, but once she looked up and gazed directly at him across the room.

The next moment he saw a tall, gray-bearded figure make his way in past the crowd by the door, and he forgot about the girl. It was Doctor Baines. Danny saw him stop and talk to a stout woman in purple, the same one who had given him punch, and then shake hands with two or three men who stopped before him. For the second time that afternoon Danny broke into a smile. He was so happy to see his old deity. Doctor Baines would be surprised to see him in uniform. Surprised and pleased, especially at how the rickety child had turned into a strong man who now filled out a uniform proudly.

Even after he recovered from his illness, Danny still saw Doctor Baines almost every afternoon for several years when Danny would help his father sell candy on the corner of the Avenue and Pecan Street after school. Doctor Baines would stroll from his office on the Avenue to the garage where he kept his automobile and stop to chat with Danny and his father. During the later years, what Danny thought of as his imprisonment in the bakery, he had not seen much of Doctor Baines, nor had he seen him before he had left for the Army. Now, he wanted to show himself off to his benefactor.

He stepped forward and asked, "Doctor Baines, remember me?"

The old man looked at him for several seconds before he exclaimed, "Danny! Danny Aramberri! What in the world!" He gave Danny a vigorous handshake and then clapped him on the shoulder. "So you're a soldier. Wonderful! How are you doing? Your family? Your father? I have missed him recently. You know, the other day I was called to Ruiz Street to see one of the Rodríguez family, Rosa, the mother, you know. She's in bad shape with pneumonia. The youngest boy is about your age; you were friends, weren't you? Well, he's in jail. First, he didn't register for his conscription, and then he got into a fight. And look at you, you certainly have turned out fine."

Danny had forgotten Doctor Baines' habit of asking questions and then not waiting for the answers. The mention of Juan Rodríguez reminded Danny of Norberto, and that he must ask Doctor Baines to help him. But Doctor Baines was already turning to greet someone else. The redheaded girl had materialized next to them, this time without the platter, and Doctor Baines was shaking her hand.

"My dear, it's so good to see you. Doing your part for the war effort, eh? Cheering up these fine boys. Good work! I am surprised, though, to see you ladies out on such a cold day as this. More credit to you. And this is one of our fine hometown boys, a patriot. Danny—Private Daniel Aramberri, U.S. Army. Miss Mary Frances Connolly."

The girl glanced briefly at Danny before dropping her eyes and blushing. Danny looked at his feet. It was awkward. They could not say that they had already met, for they had not; yet, they had already danced together. The girl looked again, this time directly at him, giving him the full benefit of a blaze of blue while taking in his clear gray eyes fringed in black, the fine bones under the pale skin, the black short-cropped hair, and smiled at what she saw.

Doctor Baines was rattling on, telling her what a sickly child Danny had been and how well and strong he looked now. Danny noticed the small pearl studs that pierced her earlobes and a wisp of lace that protruded from the handkerchief tucked inside the velvet cuff. And over the strains of a schottische, Danny heard Doctor Baines tell the girl that Manuel Aramberri was such a hardworking man, in spite of his infirmity.

"Why, he was out on the Avenue three days ago, just as the snow started to come down, and I told him to go home. I hope he didn't slip on the ice, Danny. That would be very bad for him. Now, Danny, when he was a boy, he would help his father after school. I took Danny to school, to Miss Goodman; otherwise, he might have never gone to school at all. After school, Danny would be out there with Manuel, selling the candy, and tamales sometimes too, on the Avenue and Pecan Street. You must have seen them there, I am sure. It's only a block from the Driskill Hotel, where you and your father used to live before he married your stepmother. And how is your good father, the judge? And Mrs. Connolly?"

But the girl was no longer listening. Danny, turned into stone, saw her staring distractedly across the room, without appearing to notice that her feet were already moving toward the door. She paused from her flight for a moment, and he saw her tug at her handkerchief and pull it out from inside the left sleeve, the same handkerchief that had peeped out coyly before from behind the blue velvet cuff. She was now rubbing her hands frantically with the wisp of linen and lace while a dull red flush covered her neck and her face.

Danny looked at her again and remembered from years before the young ladies and their parasols and the boys in their sailor suits stopping to buy milk candy on the Avenue, and his father carefully taking out the candy squares from the glass box and deferentially putting them in their hands. "Manuel, *el dulcero*, Manuel, the candymaker," was what he was known as by everyone who saw him standing at the corner of Pecan and the Avenue or, crab-like, slowly making his way through the streets up and down the hills, his twisted body straining under the glass box and the wooden frame that he carried on his shoulder, to complete the crustacean semblance.

Danny remembered the young girl who had once scolded her companions for buying candy from the dirty Mexicans. Didn't they know how those people lived, that they burrowed around the dump for food? And Danny had, indeed, remembered joining the Rodríguez boys when they followed the bakery van to the dump by the river and scooping up a cake that had not been all that stale. And then there was the old man who, people said, only ate what he could find in the rubble. He had been their neighbor.

He left Doctor Baines still talking and walked out the door. An icy blast of air hit him as he stepped outside, and he realized how much the room had been overheated. Where to go now? He could not bear the thought of the claustrophobic closeness of his parents' house. He realized that he had thought of it as "his parents' house" and not his own. He had been gone only six months, and it had ceased to be his home. And the city, was it still home? Is this what home is, he asked himself, where you will always be the candymaker or the candymaker's son?

He headed towards the Capitol, and when he arrived there, he found himself walking through the grounds. The park was deserted now, the children gone home for supper. The sun was low in the west, its light tinting the white-crested hills with a rosy glow. However, in the hollow where the children had played earlier out of the wind, dusk had already settled and turned the area gray and as inhospitable as a lunar crater. Once again, as on the night before, he saw his footsteps but did not hear them. Above him, the trees, with their skeletal snow-covered branches and hanging icicles, compounded the feeling of being in the middle of a dream. For a moment he forgot where he was, but, then, shaking his head, he walked south and soon stood on the front steps of the Capitol building.

From the top of the steps, past the double row of naked sycamores that lined the drive to the front entrance of the building, he could see down the length of the Avenue where the street lights were beginning to come on. It was white all the way to the river. He could not see it from where he stood, but he knew that the refuse dump was also there by the river. It, too, was decently disguised by the snow today, but he knew that the thaw would soon set in, perhaps as early as tomorrow, and then the putrefaction would resume. No matter. Tomorrow he would be gone. There was the Army, the war, the world, perhaps death too, but out there at least the odds had not been fixed yet.

Temporary Residents

Adela has known for some time that they are never going home. Her father and her sister, she thinks, have not yet come to this realization. Her father, when asked by acquaintances whether he and his family like their new residence, looks away, as if embarrassed, and says in a deprecating tone, "*Estamos de paso,*" "We are passing through."

It is true that Adela's father no longer visits the Mexican Consulate to inquire if word has come that all is well now, and that he may return to regain possession of his life and of his property. He actually only did that for about a year, when they first came, in 1914. But when the government in Mexico took a decidedly hostile turn—from Don Luis' point of view— he thought it prudent to not show himself at the Consulate anymore. After all, exiles, or temporary visitors, had met with accidents in the streets of San Antonio and of El Paso. Neither does Adela's father stop by the First National Bank anymore to see if a letter of credit has arrived from his estate administrator. All that took place in the first months, the first year or two, when their bags had still been packed, ready for the return trip home.

They have been in San Antonio for twelve years, and it is now 1926, Adela thinks distractedly, so why does Don Luis still speak of being here only temporarily, and why does Cristina still remember fondly her canaries and her plants that she left in the care of the neighbors back home?

And Luisita? Does Luisita remember the geraniums in their clay pots lining the tile-paved patio or the canaries in their cages basking in the morning sun in front of the double windows in the dining room? Luisita is such a quiet child that not even Adela, who is more her mother than her aunt, knows precisely what she remembers, or what she misses, if anything. No, not a child, Adela corrects herself. Luisita is no longer a child but a young woman of eighteen who is to be married very soon.

Adela sometimes feels like Janus, standing on the threshold, looking to the future with Luisita, sharing the past with her father and her sister. For Luisita, the memory of any other life but that which she knows now has the consistency of a dream that fades with each waking hour. For her father and Cristina, it is the past that has the consistency of reality, and the present is the dream from which they wish to awaken. But Adela knows there is no going back. When did she first realize that?

Was it six months ago, last Christmas, when their old neighbor, Doña María (who must, indeed, be getting old now), sent her annual message with wishes for a happy Christmas season and a prosperous New Year? Among the few tidbits of news that she had included was the mention that their old neighborhood had become transformed the past two or three years by the arrival of new families, including a young family from Guadalajara who now lived in the old Nava house. Adela had read that passage with the feeling of a blow to the solar plexus. Logic told her that for twelve years Doña María had not been tending to the plants and the canaries as if she expected them to return next week, so why did it hurt so much to read of strangers in their old home?

They had come to realize, early on, that their administrator was a scoundrel. His letters at the beginning had been full of plausible reasons—some perhaps even true—of why he could not remit any funds from the rents of their property: the harvest had been poor, armed marauders had destroyed the vines, squatters had taken possession of the land. The list of calamities went on. Finally, he had stopped writing. Did her father and Cristina suspect, as Adela did, that the vineyard and the warehouses, like their home, were in other hands now?

If Don Luis and Cristina are the past and Luisita is the

future, then Adela knows that she is the present. The present is the garment factory where Adela arrives every morning at seven-thirty and which she leaves at six in the evening, six days a week. It is the long, airless room, filled with the whirring of sewing machines and the chatter of forty women bending over them, just as Adela had done until last year, when she was promoted to pattern cutter. The present is a four-room frame house with a tin roof and a sagging front porch where Cristina grows her geraniums, now, and where her father sits in the evenings after the sun had gone down.

The porch opens directly into the front room, which they still call the parlor. The porch blocks off most of the light and almost all ventilation from the parlor, even though they keep the front door open most of the time. It is here in the parlor that Adela sits with Cristina and her father this evening in April, attending to the two elderly men who have been commissioned to request Luisita's hand in marriage for young Fernando Medina. It is early spring, but it is already too warm to sit in the seldom-used room under the glare of the electric bulb that hangs from the ceiling, its light attracting the moths that beat against the screen door.

Adela looks at the two men, perspiring in their suit and ties, their hats held gingerly on their knees. Don Luis has ceased to wear a coat and tie in the house; he makes do with a waistcoat in summer and a cardigan in winter. This evening he looks very distinguished in his new black coat that Adela bought for him at a discount from the factory. His black trousers with a fine gray stripe, though not new, are still in good condition. His silver-white hair is carefully combed and his moustache neatly clipped. He is a man who has always taken care of his appearance, and he continues to do so at seventy-two. His manner, however, has become quite vague now.

Adela looks around the room and finds herself longing for her old home in Saltillo and for those far away mountains. She looks at the cracked linoleum on the floor, at the faded, second-hand sofa where their visitors sit, at the cane-backed rocking chair that her father always occupies and that is transported daily from inside the house to the porch and back inside again at night, at the two kitchen chairs in which she and Cristina now sit and which have been pressed into service as parlor furniture this evening. She remembers their old home: the parlor, a spacious, oblong room with balconies overlooking the street where twenty persons could be entertained comfortably, the long table in the dining room that would seat twelve easily. She thinks angrily that that is where Luisita—who now waits nervously in the bedroom—should have grown up and had her suitors come to call.

What kind of marriage can a girl make if she lives in a frame shack? For her father, frame houses had always been shacks, although he stopped referring to them as such once they came to live here. The word now comes, unbidden, to mind. How many adjustments one has to make in a lifetime, she thinks. For her father, it would have been unthinkable twenty years ago to be receiving these two "humble but honest men" in his home, discussing with them the marriage of a member of his family.

Luisita's marriage prospects would have indeed been different back home. There is no back home, she reminds herself. Luisita is fortunate to be marrying such a hardworking, sober young man, and one who is obviously devoted to her. His family even owns a business, the small grocery store on the corner, which he will, no doubt, inherit. He is a very good match for Luisita, as good a match as could be had when marrying a Mexican here, she surprises herself by thinking. She had never thought of it that way before, never thought that being Mexican was a disadvantage; but she has to admit that being a Mexican in San Antonio, Texas, is not the same as being a Mexican at home. There is a distance, she thinks, between those two creatures that is greater than the leagues that stretch across the sunbaked vastness and across the river that separates the two. By marrying Fernando, would Luisita not become like him and those around him? But perhaps Luisita wants it that way, like a modern Ruth, saying, "Your people will be my people."

Luisita takes after her grandfather—and her mother. She has the same fair skin of porcelain flawlessness, the same blue eyes, the golden hair. The neighbors had told Adela that she could have sent Luisita to the American school and nobody would have been any wiser, but Don Luis had rejected the idea, saying that he did not want his granddaughter associating with Protestants and other foreigners. When they arrived in San Antonio, Luisita had just begun to read and write, having been a student for several months at the Academy for Young Ladies run by the señoritas Domínguez in Saltillo. In San Antonio, after an agonizing debate as to whether they would be there long enough for Luisita to enroll in school and, if so, where, Adela and Cristina had taken the child to the Academia Hidalgo for children of both sexes. This had caused Don Luis great concern until he was assured that the boys' classes did not go beyond those of ten years. The children at the Academia were, for the most part, sons and daughters of exiles like themselves, where the school director, a vague, middle-aged woman attemped to create an atmosphere of gentility. There was no denying the fact, though, that the families of solid economic means sent their daughters to the Ursuline convent while the Academia Hidalgo's fortunes had declined through the years, paralleling the diminishing means of its less fortunate patrons.

This evening in April, Cristina and Adela sit flanking their father, listening to the emissaries. The older of the two men, who always takes the lead in the conversation, has just commented on the unseasonal warmth for the second time. Then, having exhausted the topic, he pauses. Adela manages to catch Cristina's eye and signals with a nod towards the kitchen to remind Cristina that it is time to serve refreshments. Cristina hurries out of the room and returns just as the older man has resumed his comments with a tray on which rest five glasses of lemonade.

He is now saying what a good, loving son Fernando Medina is and what a good husband he will make. There is silence while the two men sip from their glasses and then pause to wipe their lips with the small embroidered napkins that

Cristina has provided. Don Luis holds his glass as if unaware of what it is doing in his hand. He seems to be staring at a point just above the speaker's shoulder. The man now begins to praise Luisita, remarking on what a virtuous, well-brought-up young lady she is, as industrious as she is beautiful; how she could have any young man she wanted for a husband; still how young Fernando is not a match to be despised, and how the elder Mr. Medina and his wife would be very honored if Don Luis would grant his granddaughter's hand in marriage to their son.

Adela stares fixedly at her father, willing him to make a suitable reply, praying that he will not utter some careless, disparaging remark. Will he say that it is out of the question, the two families are of such unequal stature, reminding them of his properties and his pedigree? Instead, he surprises Adela by turning to look at her, and there is a question and an appeal in his gaze. She gives him an almost imperceptible nod, and there is a sudden expression of bleakness and despair on his face. He stands up and thanks the guests for the honor of their visit, but he is not feeling well and must retire.

"My daughter knows my thoughts on this matter," he adds.

The two visitors look as bewildered as Cristina, but Adela takes over the discussion. Cristina is the older of the two, but the task of leading the family through the vicissitudes of the last years has fallen on Adela, seemingly by default. She now makes the major decisions without any challenge. Adela repeats her father's thanks to the two men and wants them to convey the entire family's regards to the Medina family for the honor of their request. Her father does not oppose the marriage of the young people, but, of course, Luisita must be consulted. A response will be forthcoming within the next few days. The men place their lemonade glasses on the floor, take their hats, stand up, shake hands and thank the women for their courtesy.

Luisita, of course, has known all along of the reason for the visit. It is she who has warned Adela about it after Fernando had told her of the arrangements. It is Luisita who has made the lemonade and set out the glasses and helped Cristina prepare the parlor for the visitors. She and Fernando have been courting and walking out together for over a year, since she turned seventeen, although they have known each other since they were children. Her apprehension this evening, like Adela's, comes from not knowing what her grandfather's reaction will be to the question of her marriage.

Once the visitors have gone, Adela calls out to Luisita to come out of the bedroom, which the three women share. Adela gives her a hug. Everything has happened as well as could be expected; Grandfather has raised no objections. No, he did not seem happy about it, but neither did he object. He had merely excused himself, removed himself from a distressing situation as much as he could, as he has always done throughout his life.

Don Luis has always been fortunate in having women around him who have cushioned life's blows before they reached him. First, it was his wife who had brought to the marriage sufficient property to provide a secure and comfortable existence: the vineyard and house in the country and the warehouses in town, as well as her personal talent for unobtrusive management. Then, when that good woman's heart gave out, it was Luisa, the middle and favorite daughter, who, in her charming and seemingly careless way, had provided her father with another worker bee in the person of her husband. Don Luis had not hidden his disappointment over Luisa's marriage. Luisa was not only his namesake, she also resembled him physically, and Don Luis was, perhaps justifiably so, proud of his good looks. No marriage would have been too brilliant for her, and she had chosen to marry a mere mining engineer. But Alfredo, Luisa's husband, had proven to be as useful working above ground as underneath, and the vineyard had prospered and so had the family.

Then, when tragedy struck and Luisa and Alfredo were felled by a deadly typhoid epidemic, it was young Adela's turn. She was only twenty when she stepped forward to take charge of the year-old Luisita and of overseeing the harvest until an administrator could be found. Cristina was the oldest, six years older than Adela, and on her had fallen the running of the household upon their mother's death. Perhaps for that reason she had not had time for suitors.

Cristina took after her mother in looks: the same tall, spare frame, the same long, narrow face, the same ebony black hair and eyes that she also shares with Adela. But she has little of her mother's enterprise and practical sense. These were inherited by Adela.

Within a few days of the visit, an affirmative response goes back to Mr. and Mrs. Medina in an appropriately formal note, written by Adela but signed with the name of Don Luis Nava. Adela meets with Mrs. Medina, and both ladies agree that a short engagement is best. Luisita is inclined towards a June wedding, and Sunday, June 12, is decided upon.

The next item to be decided is the bride's dress. Adela reflects that, even if Luisa's dress were available, the fashions have changed so dramatically in the twenty years or so since that wedding, that it would be out of the question for Luisita to wear her mother's dress. God only knows what has happened to that lovely confection of lace and satin that used to rest amongst tissue paper in the big cedar chest of the guest bedroom. Had the new inhabitants of their house taken possession of it? Or had the family barely been gone when neighbors and strangers alike looted the house of its contents under cover of the general violence that pervaded their lives? It is futile to speculate, Adela tells herself. Even if they were ever to return, the fate of a wedding dress or a set of china would hardly concern anyone, when the fate of so many lives is still unknown.

It is a good thing that dresses are short and simple now, Adela thinks, and not the long, complicated affairs with ruffles and delicate embroideries they used to be. Although Adela is a good seamstress, she would not have been able to produce—or afford—such a dress. Fernando's family, in keeping with tradition, has provided an adequate gift of money for Luisita's trousseau. In the past, this custom could sometimes lead to touchy situations, as when the bride's family had the greater wealth, in which case the bridegroom's gift to his fiancée became a mere token or symbol. But there is no question now of Luisita's family being able to furnish her entire trousseau, and the gift goes towards purchasing household necessities, such as dishes and linens. Luisita will embroider the linens with her initials: "M.L.E." for María Luisa Escalante." The wedding dress, however, is provided by Adela and Cristina, who have scraped together their savings and bought a length of silk, again at a discount from the factory, and which they will sew themselves as their wedding gift to Luisita.

There is also a wedding quilt to be made. Here the lack of parlor furniture turns out to be a benefit, for all they have to do is push the sofa out of the way and set up the quilting frame. Wool is procured and carded for the batting, and a design is drawn on the cotton sateen for stitching: garlands of flowers, since Cristina has vetoed the lyre pattern as bringing bad luck to brides.

Luisita is a good needlewoman; indeed, she helps Cristina with the fine embroidery they do at home for hire. While Adela works at the garment factory, Cristina and Luisita sew at home as well, smocking fine children's clothes, embroidering christening robes and fine bed linens, both by hand and on the second-hand sewing machine which they acquired soon after moving into the house. It pains Adela to see the young girl hard at work at such an early age. Luisita has not had the music lessons that Adela and her sisters had when they were growing up, nor has she had the time or the opportunity to read much literature or engage in the diversions and amusements that her aunts had grown up with. But perhaps all those things belong to another time, another place.

Adela had hoped that Luisita would attend commercial college, learn typing and shorthand, as well as English, as she herself would have liked to do. She would have liked to see Luisita working in an office, if she had to work at all. Luisita has such a sweet disposition, such nice manners and a refined appearance. But Luisita's studies ended six years after they had started, when she reached twelve; and the precarious existence of the Academia Hidalgo had, likewise, come to an end soon after that. Luisita had learned to read and write with very nice penmanship, had studied a little history and geography of the world and "notions of arithmetic and geometry," as the director had put it. These subjects had exhausted the store of knowledge of the director and her sister, the only two teachers for the fifty children or so at the Academia.

The entire curriculum had been in Spanish, of course, since the idea at the time of the founding of the school, in 1913, had been that the children's attendance there would constitute a mere hiatus in their lives before returning home. Their parents did not want them to remain idle or ignorant while they waited for the political situation in Mexico to sort itself out, so they sent them to school. These were the children of the middle and the upper middle classes. The children of the poor fared no better than their parents: schooling was out of the question for them. The truly rich always made provisions ahead of time for living abroad and did not have to pinch pennies to pay for tuition, as Luisita's family had done.

From the beginning, paying for Luisita's tuition had proven to be a sacrifice almost beyond her family's ability to make, and, finally, it had become impossible, no matter how low the fees were. Indeed, the tuition fees for the school were absurdly low, and for that reason, no doubt, the school had failed.

In fact, by 1920 Don Luis Nava's family was at the end of its tether where it concerned finances. The small sums which the administrator had sporadically remitted at first had ceased to arrive some two years before. The heirlooms which they had managed to smuggle out with them had been sold, including their mother's diamond earrings—but not her wedding ring, thank God. There simply was no money to pay for any kind of schooling for Luisita, and at the end of the school year in June, they informed the director that Luisita would not be coming back. The señorita Bocanegra, looking more lugubrious than ever, told them that she understood; other families were in the same predicament. The predicament was hers, too, for the school did not reopen the following year. As for Luisita, she stayed home from then on and helped Cristina and Adela with the housework and freeing them for work that paid.

The question of a job had been a delicate one from the very first. Don Luis would have been horrified at the thought of his daughters hiring themselves out as employees to anybody. He, himself, was already in his sixties, and what could he do? The chief expertise of this displaced former man of property was a knowledge of the social graces required of a gentleman. Cristina's skills were purely domestic, but to work as a servant was unthinkable. Adela, who had kept accounts of rents and expenses and had dealt with administrators and workmen, found herself at a disadvantage in a foreign place, with no connections and no knowledge of English. One could get by very well within one's own circle of acquaintances with only Spanish, but the language of business and commerce and the law was English.

Both Cristina and Adela had learned fine needlework as children, and through a friend, another expatriate like themselves, they began to get work embroidering fancy table linens. They were paid by the piece and were furnished all the materials. Don Luis never caught on—or if he did, he did not let on—that his daughters' frenzied needlework was being done for pay. If he wondered what happened to those stacks of linen after his daughters finished with them, he never asked. Eventually, Luisita came to help with the needlework as well, at first simply doing odd jobs such as snipping stray threads and folding the linens carefully after they were done. Gradually, she mastered the various stitches, and Adela had to admit that the young girl had a greater talent for this work than she did.

As they sat at their embroidery, Adela would sometimes remember those first chaotic months of their exile that led them to the unlikely haven of the little frame house where they lived now. The first year in San Antonio had been a nightmare. They rented two rooms in the Flores boardinghouse. During that entire time, Don Luis had complained of the noise made by the other boarders and of the food, which was truly bad. Adela felt like a hunted creature, hounded by both her father's demands and their own precarious finances.

They were lured to the Flores boardinghouse by a newspaper advertisement that proclaimed the virtues of the establishment in terms of "a family ambience of the highest respectability with home-cooked meals." Upon arriving at the address given in the newspaper, they found a large house with a long veranda, with brick showing where the overlay of stucco had peeled off. Don Luis had been reassured when he saw that it was a masonry house; he had a fear of fire in woodframe houses, of which there seemed to be many in San Antonio. The landlady received them with great amiability. It would be an honor for her to have as guests persons of such obvious distinction. She then praised the merits of the house, emphasizing its utmost respectability and the high caliber of her guests. They would receive three meals a day, she said, "Home-style cooking, nothing fancy, but so tasty and nourishing. . ." Laundry was also included in the rent. She went on to tell them that the house had been in the family of her dear, departed husband almost since the founding of San Antonio. "They were Canary Islanders, you know, the founders." Don Luis was convinced. The landlady's forceful personality, coupled with the lure of the history embodied by the house was too strong a mixture for him to resist. They went back to the Menger Hotel, settled their account and moved out.

They had been at the Menger for two weeks, and Adela had reached a stage of frenzied distraction at the thought of how fast their money would run out if they stayed there much longer. When they arrived in San Antonio, Don Luis had asked the train porter which was the best hotel in town, and the porter had directed them to the Menger. It had, indeed, been very pleasant and comfortable, and had provided the wonderful balm of tranquility after the nightmarish days and nights on the road, but Adela dreaded the expense. It was not as if they were well-to-do tourists on an excursion abroad. The money they had been able to bring out with them would have to last through all sorts of contingencies. These thoughts did not seem to unduly preoccupy Don Luis, though, and it was only because American food did not agree with him that Adela was able to convince him to move into a place where people would cater to his taste. And so they had moved into the Flores establishment, although, as Don Luis explained to his landlady, it would probably be for only a few weeks.

The weeks stretched into months during which Don Luis discovered that eating your own cuisine is no great boon if the food is poorly prepared or made with inferior ingredients. However, if one complained that dinner had been burned or almost inedible, the señora Flores would immediately take the attitude that "everyone tries to take advantage of a poor helpless widow." This attitude was at variance, with the flint-like hardness of her eyes and of her heart.

Neither did the architecture or the history of the house make up for living in two small rooms at the back where the sun hardly ever shone. The small, dark quarters and the proximity to their unpleasant landlady drove Adela outdoors and into the street for long walks around the city. Don Luis did not approve of her solitary meanderings, but she was beyond caring. She would go to the commercial district and look in the shop windows at the merchandise displayed trying to decipher the advertisements written in English. She walked past barber shops and restaurants of various nationalities, where men loitered at the doors. She even ventured into the busy produce market, stepping gingerly to keep out of the way of the shirtsleeved men who ran to and fro unloading great crates of fruits and vegetables. The customers milled about, oblivious to the activity around them, concentrating on their own purchases. There were fierce-looking hotel cooks in white aprons, small merchants, boardinghouse landladies and housewives with baskets hanging from their arms. Once when she spied their own landlady, rummaging through a bin of wilted cabbages; Adela decided to forgo dinner that day.

At the periphery of the market were the Mexican street vendors with tamales and candy. She usually made a purchase from them or stopped at a bakery nearby for coffee and bread from home. The aroma of the fresh bread and the sound of Spanish around her filled her with comfort, so that she could return to face again their cheerless quarters.

While she was out she would also purchase a newspaper. She read in *La Prensa* that thousands of refugees from the Mexican Revolution, like herself and her family, were now residing in San Antonio. That fact itself made possible the publication of the Spanish-language newspaper, also published by exiles. She learned to recognize other expatriates like herself as distinct from the native Texas-Mexicans. The expatriates acknowledged each other as long-lost friends in the midst of strangers. Even walking down the street they recognized each other and exchanged smiles, struck up conversations, which would have been unthinkable with anybody else without prior introduction.

They were strangers in a strange land and had to stand together. Although it was not such a strange land after all, they told themselves. They were in Texas, which had once been part of Mexico, and in spite of the influx of Anglo Americans, much of Mexico still remained. Look at the name of the town; look at the names of the people; look at how many of the old customs were still retained. And they consoled themselves with the thought that they were not in a foreign country after all.

As she got to know the city better, Adela became bolder and wandered further afield. It was in this manner that she came across the small white frame house with the sign that read, *"Se renta."* It was obviously a Mexican neighborhood and poor, like most of them, but the houses were neatly kept. She eventually tracked down the person whose name was given in the advertisement and made arrangements to view the house. She had come to the conclusion that, if she and Cristina could do their own marketing and cook their own food, they could live cheaper than with the Widow Flores. They would certainly eat better.

Adela took Cristina with her to see the house. It was owned by another widow, Nicolasa Cadena, and if she was blunt in stating her terms, she had none of the affectations of their current landlady. They agreed to take the house, and then went to tell their father of their decision. Don Luis was unusually docile and acquiesced to the move without much protest. The enforced fasts in the boardinghouse had taken their toll on his health and on his spirit; not even his fear of fire caused him to balk at moving into a frame house. After all, it was only a temporary arrangement.

Ten years later, they were still in the same house. The neighborhood was quite modest, most of its inhabitants being laborers, with the exception of a few small business owners, such as the Medina family, who lived in the second story of the building that housed their grocery store. Within the surrounding blocks, there was also a bakery and a shop where they repaired and upholstered furniture and whose owners likewise resided on the premises.

At first the members of Don Luis Nava's household did not associate with their neighbors. Even Luisita was kept aloof from the neighborhood children, a situation reinforced by the fact that Luisita attended the Academia while the neighborhood children went to school, if they went at all, in a dilapidated building some eight or nine blocks away that was known as the "Mexican School." Class distinctions, however, did not preclude courtesy, Don Luis maintained, and he was always ready when he went out with greetings and salutations. As for the rest of the family, proximity simply wore down barriers, and gradually Luisita began playing with the neighborhood children in the street where they all gathered for their games. Cristina and Adela, for their part, would stop to chat with other women in the grocery store or stand, like their neighbors, in the front yard in the evening and converse with the passers-by about the heat or the lack of rain or the progress of their gardens.

Those first years, before they became acclimatized, they all suffered intensely from the heat. After a life in the cool, dry air of the mountains, the Texas summers overwhelmed them. Don Luis, being older, suffered the most. In the middle of the summer, he would get dizzy spells, which he blamed on the poor construction of the house—its low ceilings and tin roof, in particular, that trapped the heat inside. To his dismay, he found that he could no longer wear a coat and tie at home in July and August, and he traded his lace-up boots for carpet slippers, as well.

As time went by, their contacts with home dwindled. They seldom received letters now, and Don Luis, trying to make sense of the situation in Mexico, where outright civil war raged on, read *La Prensa* for news from the front. The United States had sent in troops to Mexico to pursue Pancho Villa. Don Luis, to whom Villa was nothing but a barbarian, was nevertheless outraged by the American intervention. He feared it was the end of the country. The Americans were going to take now what they had not taken in 1848.

Then the United States entered the European war, and Villa was forgotten, his place taken by the Kaiser as the archvillain in the public's mind. Now they read *La Prensa* for news about the war in Europe, as well as the war back home. And then there were the Bolsheviks in Russia. When news of the murders of the Czar and his family came, Don Luis grieved over them as if they had been his own royal family. In that way, discussion of world events filled the void in their shipwrecked existence.

Then the war in Europe was over, and a sort of peace descended over Mexico as well, more out of exhaustion than because of any clear victory by any side. The country lay in shambles. Violence, however, hid just under the surface, as when after a fire has burned itself out the embers still smolder under the ashes, ready to flare up again if fuel is added. Most of the exiles knew this and were afraid to return, even those who had something to return to. Don Luis and his family did not know if they did. All correspondence from home had ceased, and their administrator—former administrator, surely by now—was not to be found. They decided to wait a little longer before attempting a return trip. After all, when they had left, some five years before, there had been an order outstanding for the arrest of Don Luis Nava on grounds of conspiring against the government. No general amnesty had been issued yet for political refugees.

After the World War, everything seemed to cost more than before. The Widow Cadena, who had proven to be a better landlady than the refined señora Flores, informed them reluctantly that she had to increase the rent. Some of the increase would go to making deferred repairs to the house. Adela was only too conscious of the need for repairing the roof, but had been aware, as well, that the repair would entail an increase in the rent and had foregone asking for it. At this point, Adela felt that she was getting in deep water, and that a change had to be made.

With Luisita helping out at home, Adela decided that she could be spared to look for a job outside. What kind of job she could get, she did not know, for she had no formal training, and language was still a barrier. She had begun to make it a point to buy, when she could afford it, the American newspapers and tried to read them with the aid of an English-Spanish dictionary. She had achieved some success in reading English this way, but the spoken word still eluded her. Then, at the grocery store, she heard that jobs for women were to be had at a garment factory recently opened, and without giving herself time to reconsider, she marched down to the location indicated.

When she arrived at the factory she wondered how she would make herself understood, but the foreman seemed prepared for this contingency, for he interviewed her in broken Spanish, which was adequate for the information he required. Could she operate a sewing machine? Yes, she could. What was her name, address, age and marital status? Her answers satisfied him, and he told her to present herself the following morning at work.

Dazed by her quick success, she, nevertheless, realized that she had to break the news to her father. She went straight home and told him without preambles that she had taken a job and where. She was too tired for circumlocutions and embellishments this time; she told him bluntly that their situation was becoming desperate and that her salary could make the difference between becoming destitute and being able to continue living in their modest circumstances. She had never seen such despair on his face before, and, as if to hide it, he turned his head away from her. He looked at his hands, still white and slender but now starting to be mottled by age. When he spoke, his voice trembled, but all he said was, "I have brought you all to this." She could not think of any response to make.

At first, working in the factory was harder than anything else she had done before. Bending over the sewing machine for ten hours a day with only a half hour for a hasty lunch, day after day, under the harsh glare of the overhead lights, she sometimes felt that her neck and shoulder muscles were one throbbing mass of pain. With time and practice, however, her muscles relaxed, and she found that the camaraderie of the twenty-odd women that worked with her softened the harshness of the work. The improvement in their financial situation also made for peace of mind, and she began to plan to put aside money so Luisita could go to commercial college and learn bookkeeping and English. This was not to be. Don Luis developed a severe bronchitis and required medical care; then, while convalescing, he experienced chest pains that led the doctor to believe that his patient had angina. The pains eventually went away, and he was completely recovered by the following spring; but in order to pay the doctor and buy medicine, Adela had had to borrow money, which she spent the following year paying back.

At work, Adela increased her circle of acquaintances and friends. They were mostly young, unmarried girls in their twenties that worked with her, as well as a few women in their thirties, like Adela herself, and several widows, including two war widows. They were all Spanish speakers. Five were Mexican expatriates like herself and another was a Cuban whose former husband, a Frenchman had left her stranded in San Antonio after absconding with her money.

During the lunch break, the high-ceiling room reverberated with their chatter and their laughter as they talked about themselves or their families or made plans for Sunday. Sometimes they asked Adela to accompany them on their Sunday outings. She usually declined, not out of any sense of superiority, but simply because by Sunday she was so tired that her greatest pleasure was to just stay home. As a rare treat, though, Adela, Cristina and Luisita would go to a moving picture on Sunday afternoon.

On a few special occasions, they even convinced Don Luis to take them all to the Teatro Nacional to watch a touring company from Mexico City present a *zarzuela*—for he was very fond of musical theater—or see a play by one of the better known nineteenth-century Spanish dramatists, who were his favorites. He would agree to go to these functions saying that he did it only to provide them with an escort, but he enjoyed himself at these events more than any of them. He was in his element here, at a theater or a salon, exchanging bows with the leading members of the Mexican colony, whom he did not see otherwise.

At the Casino Mexicano, too, which he was too poor to join, he was happy. Although they were not members, they sometimes went to the Casino as guests, particularly for the major cultural events, such as those to celebrate Independence Day in September. For him, though, the poetry readings and the musical recitals were not the main attraction of these soirees. It was, rather, the opportunity to put on his best black suit, his silver-striped tie and the diamond stick pin that otherwise reposed in its velvet case among his handkerchiefs.

He easily overshadowed his daughters. He still cut such a distinguished figure, with his straight back and his glittering blue eyes, proudly giving his arm to his pretty granddaughter. It was as if, like Cinderella, he was transformed for the ball. Adela and Cristina would follow in the wake of the old man and the young girl, neither woman concerned with more than presenting a suitable appearance—Cristina in a frock of salmon pink, a color that someone had told her, long ago, favored brunettes but did nothing for her in middle age, and Adela in severe navy blue.

It was on Luisita that the aunts lavished their attention, choosing for her various shades of light blue to bring out her eyes and her blonde hair. She was not a beauty like her mother had been. Luisa's eyes had been ablaze with a color and a fire of their own; she had been blessed as well with a complexion that brought to mind the clichés of roses on snow, and her hair of burnished gold had truly been a crown of glory. Everything in Luisita was subdued, from her eyes where the blue seemed to fade into gray to the delicate pallor of her cheeks, but she had a sweetness that her more spirited mother had lacked.

At the Casino, Adela would find herself looking around, like any anxious mother, thinking, "Perhaps Luisita will meet a suitable young man here." But then she would reproach herself, because she knew that Luisita was already keeping company with young Fernando Medina and was very fond of him. It was not that Fernando was not a good boy; he was a sober, hardworking young man and a good son, and very fond of Luisita. It was—and she would hate herself for the thought—that he was not of her class. "Forget those notions," she would tell herself, "we are all the same here now." But she did not really believe it, not yet. She knew that her father never would.

Adela has finished hemming up Luisita's wedding dress this Saturday afternoon, the eve of Luisita's wedding. Luisita and Cristina are in church, arranging the flowers on the altar for tomorrow's wedding Mass. The dress is a simple satin shift delicately embroidered with crystal beads along the neckline. Adela holds it up in front of her for a moment, standing before the half-moon mirror of the dresser, the only new piece of furniture in the house. The dress is so small that it would not fit over Adela's solid frame. Adela's neck and shoulder muscles have hardened with the years and hard work; her once slender waist has thickened from too many hours of sitting in front of a sewing machine. The face above the dress is still unlined, but the black hair, worn parted in the middle and gathered in a knot at the nape, is beginning to be streaked with gray. Her eyes, dark and wide as before, have not lost their lustre, but there is a somber expression in them now. She does not look like a bride, she thinks, peering at her face above the wedding dress.

Twelve years ago she had been ready to be the bride of Gustavo Alaniz, even without a wedding dress. It had been Gustavo who, twelve years ago, on that fateful night in February, had come to warn them, at peril to his own safety, that a warrant had been issued for Don Luis' arrest. Don Luis' name had surfaced as one of several sympathizers with the plotters who had brought about President Madero's downfall and death. Don Luis' role in the affair had been very small— just a matter of letters that had fallen into the wrong hands and a loan of money to one of the instigators of the coup. Don Luis had no more talent for political intrigue than he had for business, and his involvement was soon discovered.

He had been a reluctant conspirator. He had had no liking for Madero, personally; he called him a traitor to his class. After all, how could the scion of such a prominent family bring about a revolution and destroy the legitimate order of things? Don Luis had yearned for the return of that old order, but never did he advocate murder and violence as the means to do so. He had merely wanted to send Madero back to Paris to respectable exile, where he could join the old dictator that he had overthrown. Then things could return to their rightful place, under new, younger leaders, perhaps, but, nonetheless, men who knew right from wrong. Instead, chaos, violence and another rebellion had followed within months of Madero's assassination, and Don Luis had been prostrated with horror and disbelief.

Gustavo had friends in the revolutionary army who, knowing of his connection with the Nava family, had warned him that the order for Don Luis' arrest had been issued and that it would be served within a day or two. If Don Luis were arrested and found guilty of treason—and with the evidence of the letters and confessions already given, his guilt was a foregone conclusion—he would be shot, and his family would be exposed to the gravest danger, Gustavo said. They had to leave the city and the country immediately. Fortunately, the border was not far away. Don Luis had sat mute and immobilized by shock. It was Adela, the only other participant at the interview, who had turned to Gustavo and said, "You must tell us what to do." And he had. He told them to gather all the cash they had available and all the jewelry and hide it about their persons.

"Do not take any more clothes than you would take for a two-week stay," he said, "Tell everyone that you are going to Monterrey for a few weeks, so Don Luis can consult an eye specialist there. I will tell my mother to look after the house when you are gone," he added, "but no one must know that you are going to the border."

She had to tell Cristina, of course, and Cristina had a fainting spell and had to be revived with rubbing alcohol on the temples and wrists.

"What are we going to tell the maids?" she wailed, "and what about my plants? And the canaries . . . what is going to happen to my canaries? They will die without care." At this point Cristina had threatened to faint again, and Adela had shaken her roughly.

"We'll pay the maids two-weeks wages in advance, and then we'll send word—once we are safe—that they are free to leave. Doña María can look after the canaries and the plants after the maids are gone. We won't be gone that long, I'm sure. This is all bound to be a misunderstanding that will be cleared up. Gustavo will clear it up, you'll see."

After the show of fortitude with everyone else, that evening when she was alone in her room, Adela had broken down and cried like a frightened child. She did not want to leave her home, the only one she had ever known, sneaking off like a fugitive. And Gustavo, what would happen to her and Gustavo? Ever since she could remember, at least since she was fifteen, she had known that she was going to marry him. They had known each other since childhood; they were the same age, and their mothers were cousins. She had waited for him more than ten years—first, for him to become interested in girls and to notice her, then for him to finish his medical studies in Mexico City and come home. She was twenty-six, and he had just come home.

Don Luis had always maintained that he did not approve

of long engagements for young ladies. They wasted a girl's time and caused her to miss out on opportunities to make a good match. This was the reason he had given for withholding his consent to Adela's engagement while Gustavo was a student. The actual reason for his position was that he was in no hurry for his daughters to marry anyone at all. He preferred to have them looking after him rather than after another man. In addition to pure selfishness, he had also disapproved of his wife's cousin's marriage. Gustavo's mother, in Don Luis' estimation, had married beneath her when she had married Pepe Alaniz, who sold patent medicines and hair tonics behind a shop counter. It was Pepe's own shop, but no matter. Don Luis did not like to be related, even if only by marriage, to Pepe the druggist, as he was known. It was clearly a misalliance from the point of view of a man like Don Luis, who claimed to descend from Captain Francisco de Urdiñola, the colonizer of Nueva Vizcaya.

Don Luis' dislike of Pepe Alaniz had extended to his son, and this dislike was only slightly modified by the promising medical career that Gustavo seemed to have before him. To now owe perhaps his life to Gustavo made the gratitude harder to bear.

Adela never told anyone of how she had sobbed alone in her room while she packed her clothes that evening in February. Nor had she told what followed. Tears had not comforted her. She had become angry at her father for his stupidity; she had been filled with hatred for all those faceless people that she would never know but whose actions now shattered her entire life. Then she knew that she could not leave Gustavo. To have loved him for so long and to have waited for so many years, only to be separated again, was an agony of frustration that she could not tolerate.

Adela slipped out of her house unseen to stand in the shadows outside Gustavo's house until she saw him come home. She intercepted him and told him then that she had decided to stay, that she would not leave him. His surprise was complete. She could not possibly do that, he explained. He was joining Carranza's army within a week; they needed doctors in the battlefield. She would go with him wherever he went, become a camp follower if need be, she had told him, throwing her arms around him, begging him to keep her with him. She had felt his dismay in the stiffening of his muscles as she pressed close to him. She loved him, she kept saying, didn't he love her?

Pulling her arms away from around him, he said, yes, he loved her, and for that reason he could not expose her to the horrors and deprivations that he would endure. When it was all over, when he could offer her a home, they would be married. He insisted that she return to her house before her absence was noticed and walked back with her, reassuring her. He would write to her whenever he could; Adela could write to him in care of his mother; she would forward her letters to him. But they must be very careful; her father and all his family were in grave danger.

Adela never saw him again. After they had been in San Antonio for several weeks, she wrote to him and to his mother under separate cover. Before his mother she kept up the fiction of her father's visit to an eye specialist, a famous one to be found in San Antonio, Texas, and circumspectly gave "General Delivery" as their return address. To him she poured out her heart, telling him of her longings and her misery.

Adela had five letters from him during the first four years, short messages dashed off from cities where the army was resting and taking care of the wounded. He was always exhausted, so many wounded to care for with so little. After 1918, she did not hear from him again. From Doña María, their old neighbor, she heard that both his parents had died during the influenza epidemic of 1918, and for a time she feared that he had died as well. Adela had no way of finding out since he was an only child, and there was no one else to contact and ask of his whereabouts. In 1920, she heard that he was alive but had not returned to Saltillo; he was in charge of a military hospital in Veracruz. Finally, four years ago, in 1922, Doña María's Christmas letter brought the news that Gustavo Alaniz, now a brilliant surgeon, had returned to his home and brought with him a young bride. And that had been the end of that. Not even a letter to tell her that he was getting married. That must be what it is like when you die, she thinks now. Your memory fades from people's thoughts until they never think of you again. And then you are truly dead. Adela shakes her head and tells herself that the eve of Luisita's wedding is no time for morbid thoughts. She lays down the bride's dress on the bed, wraps it in tissue paper and places the veil and the simple wreath of orange blossoms next to it. It is too bad that the orange blossoms are made of wax, but even if one could find orange trees this far north, it is past their season for blooming.

On the wedding day, there is no time for meditation. All rise at five, while it is still dark, and the two women help the bride to dress before dressing themselves. Luisita is pale but composed. Don Luis looks distinguished in his black suit and is wearing a new tie, bought for the occasion. His silver hair gleams, his white shirt is stiff with starch. At six-thirty, the hired car takes them all to church.

There are some fifty persons in the wedding party, almost all friends or relatives of the bridegroom, although many are also neighbors of the bride. There are only four or five members of the "Mexican Colony," as the expatriates call themselves, present in the bride's party. Many of them have already begun to return to Mexico, among them those closest to the Navas. Two or three of Adela's closest co-workers are also there. The rest of the people that fill the church are regular parishioners attending Sunday Mass who, nonetheless, enjoy the happy spectacle of a wedding.

Luisita and her grandfather walk up the aisle to the altar, arm in arm, to the organ strains of the wedding march. At the altar rail Don Luis steps back, and Fernando takes his place at Luisita's side. The couple kneels down on silk cushions that have been provided by the *padrinos,* Fernando's aunt and uncle who, along with the other wedding sponsors, sit in the front pews.

The Mass begins and, as the minutes go by, Adela worries that Luisita is too pale. They are all fasting in order to receive Communion, and she fears that Luisita might faint.

But, no, the marriage ceremony proper has begun, and Luisita answers in a firm voice that she takes Fernando as her husband and receives from him a ring and the gold coins that signify that he endows her with all his worldly goods. The priest is now giving a short homily on Christian love and congratulating the couple. It is all going so fast, Adela thinks—the wedding mass, the last twelve years. Now the newlyweds are leaving the church while the organ plays the recessional, and the wedding party poses for photographs outside the church.

Adela and Cristina do not pause for photographs. They rush back to the house where several tables covered with white tablecloths are set up in the parlor and the kitchen. The extra tables and chairs and even some of the pastries for the wedding breakfast have been furnished by helpful neighbors. The wedding party arrives just as Adela and Cristina have finished setting out pitchers of hot chocolate and platters laden with the traditional wedding shortbread cut in heart shapes and rolled in sugar and cinnamon.

The small house is soon crowded, and some of the men and the younger people stay on the porch and let the elders and the immediate family of the couple be served first. Adela worried about leaving her father to return home on his own, but she sees him arrive with Fernando's parents. They are all being very kind to him, but the old man, in spite of his straight back and his air of being somebody, looks lost in his own home. Luisita takes his arm and leads him to the head of the table in the parlor. She and Fernando sit by him, and the rest of the table is taken by the older members of the Medina family.

Adela does not have time to converse with anyone as she hurries from the kitchen to the parlor, refilling cups and bringing fresh pastries, even a plate of hot tamales delivered just then by a neighbor. "How kind everyone is," she thinks, almost with surprise, and then she notices her father, his cup half-full and cooling, his hand nervously crumbling a piece of bread on the tablecloth and a look on his face of wishing he were somewhere else. She feels a sudden rush of anger.

"Please, God," she prays, "Don't let him spoil his granddaughter's wedding. Don't let him offend her new family."

Adela's attention is diverted by the arrival of a very old man who pauses at the door, supported by one of the couples who had been padrinos. Adela helps them install the old man at the other end of the table, opposite from Don Luis, and she brings him chocolate. The old man is the bridegroom's great-grandfather; he is ninety-two.

"Amazing, how he is so alert and has all his wits intact," remarks the old man's middle-aged granddaughter. "It is only his hearing and his rheumatism that bother him."

Adela leaves them and goes to the kitchen to refill her pitcher. Cristina is in there, frantically twirling the wooden whisk between her hands to whip up froth in another batch of chocolate. They do not speak; the elder sister merely hands the younger one another pitcher of chocolate. From the kitchen door Adela sees that Luisita is leading her grandfather to the other end of the table and hurries after them with the frank purpose of eavesdropping on the introduction. Luisita is saying, "Papá Luisito, this is Fernando's..." she pauses, blushing, "my husband's great-grandfather, Don Domingo Rodríguez. He was born in one of the houses close to the river and remembers what San Antonio was like even before the Anglo-Americans came."

Turning to the old man and raising her voice, she completes the introductions. "Don Domingo, this is my grandfather, Don Luis Nava."

The old man looks at Don Luis without great interest and nods his head briefly. His granddaughter, Fernando's aunt, interjects brightly, like a hostess trying to get the conversation going, to her grandfather, "*Abuelo*, Don Luis and his family come from Mexico, from the mountains close to Monterrey." Don Luis flinches with momentary annoyance to hear his hometown so glibly merged with its rival city. "But you have lived here for some time now, haven't you?" she continues, a little archly.

Adela, pitcher poised in midair, stares fixedly at her father and would mouth the words for him to utter, but he forestalls her.

"Yes," he says, addressing both the woman and the old man, "we came from far away, but that was a long time ago. We live in San Antonio now. This is our home . . . and yours," he adds the courteous formula.

*

Late that night Adela lies awake in her bed while the moonlight streams in through the uncurtained window, and Cristina snores in her bed against the opposite wall. She is too tired to sleep. The day was hectic, the bride's wedding breakfast having been followed by the *almuerzo* at the bridegroom's home. The second meal, more a dinner than a luncheon, was attended by many more guests than the breakfast, in keeping with the groom's family's ampler house and ampler means.

The music and the dancing had continued well into dusk, but Don Luis had retired home in the early afternoon. Adela had also left early to finish packing Luisita's suitcase. The sun was setting when the newlyweds came by. Luisita changed out of her wedding clothes and prepared to leave with her husband. Only then did the girl cry as she embraced her two aunts. Then she and Fernando were gone.

In bed, Adela thinks that she should cry too, now, when it is all over and she can do so. She looks at the narrow cot that Luisita will occupy no more and thinks that she should be sad. But, strangely, she is not. Luisita and Fernando are in their new home, only a few blocks away. She will see them every day, or as often as she likes, anyway. That is how things should be.

How pleased she was with her father's response this morning. He had not rebuffed their guests' kind interest with the usual evasion of being a temporary visitor. She was surprised at the time and wondered if he was simply opting for a courteous lie in making their city his own. But perhaps he was speaking the truth. How long is it, Adela asks herself, since he has remembered the old days and spoken of the old home and the old ways? How long ago is it since Cristina got the canary that now sleeps in its shrouded cage in the kitchen? Adela suddenly feels like the lone mourner after everyone else has forgotten a death. Perhaps it is time for her to forget as well.

Agnus Dei

T he call came in at 5:03 P.M., according to the emergency medical services dispatcher. This did not mean that it happened at 5:03. It might have happened at 5:00, or even at 4:55. Not much earlier than that, though, because someone had called the ambulance almost immediately. Most likely it had happened at five o'clock. On the dot. *En punto.* Like that bullfighter's death in the poem by Lorca that Al had read in Spanish class in college. A frightening poem, he had always thought.

But five o'clock was only the culmination of events. So . . . when had it begun? When had the combination of events first been set in motion? Was it some five hours earlier, at noon, when Eduardo left the bicycle at the pharmacy and went home with his mother in the car? Was it when his mother said to the boy, "Leave it here and get in the car. You can pick it up later. Lunch will get cold if we don't hurry up"?

Olga had left a styrofoam container with his favorite dish of chicken stewed with summer squash for him to eat at work and took three other containers home for her, for Eduardo and for Gloria, who was visiting at home that day. On Saturdays, Olga would usually pick up some breakfast or lunch at the Nuevo León restaurant to take home. The Nuevo León was two blocks away from the pharmacy and six blocks from the house. A neighborhood place, unpretentious, with some real home cooking, not that phony stuff that tourists thought was Mexican food, all gooey yellow cheese and grease. Was it then that it had all started, when they had fallen into the habit of stopping by the Nuevo León on Saturdays?

Was it when the boy had decided to stop at the Insta-mart to buy a soft drink? Was it when he stopped to talk to a friend on the sidewalk on the way home? If he had not stopped to talk, if he had not been delayed for those few minutes, would he have avoided his fateful meeting with death? If he had not been distracted later by the bottle of soda pop in his hand as he sat back on the seat, the bicycle going only fast enough to remain upright? Would it have happened? If those thugs had not decided to shoplift a couple of six-packs of beer and make a run for it, if a sixteen-year old had not already been drunk when he got behind the wheel of the car that he did not have a license to drive, if the Instamart did not sell beer, if they had not lived in the kind of neighborhood where an Instamart nestled cheek to jowl with homes, if they had not lived in the sort of neighborhood that had juvenile thugs that got drunk on Saturday afternoon—would any of it have happened?

If Eduardo had been at the mall with his mother and his sister, or at the movies with his friends, or if he had gone to summer camp like his classmates at school, would it have happened then? Or was it already preordained? When he was born, was it there already in his future that the first fourteenth of June after his twelfth birthday would mark the end? Was it also preordained that it should be at five o'clock in the afternoon, five o'clock on a hot summer afternoon?

If Al took the day's events, hour by hour, if he rearranged the hours, like cards in a deck, would he learn which, among them, was the fateful hour? If Eduardo had come home with his mother, if Al, his father, had stayed at the pharmacy till closing time and not taken off early to get his hair cut at Mike's Barber Shop, which was only four blocks from the pharmacy and which he had patronized since he was a boy, would any of that have changed the outcome?

Al had been sitting in the barber's chair, and Mike was sprinkling talcum powder on the nape of his neck and brushing away the remaining hair clippings from under his collar. He was wondering how the Astros were going to do this year while Mike talked about Fernando Valenzuela's pitching,

when ten-year-old Art Flores came in running from the
street, very pale and out of breath and said, "Mr. Estrada,
oh, Mr. Estrada, Eduardo has been hurt; a car hit him." He
was at once out of the chair, scattering the towel and clip-
pers, shouting, "Where?"

"About half a block from the Instamart."

He almost took off running then, but realized the next
moment that he had the car and that it would be faster to
drive even those few blocks, if only he could stop shaking and
be able to get the key in the ignition. Mike came out running
after him, telling the customers inside to hold the fort until
he got back. Mike took the keys from him and said, "Get in,
Al. I will drive you."

Mike had been in high school with him and, before that,
in elementary school. Their classmates used to say that
Mike was bound to be a barber, even if his father had not
already owned a barber shop—he liked talking so much. He
kept talking in the car—monotonous, meaningless words,
first in Spanish and then in English—to comfort him and
keep him from jumping out of the car and running dement-
edly down the street. "He's going to be all right. He'll be all
right, you'll see. It's only bruises, scratches. He's going to be
all right."

And he had almost believed that Mike was right when he
first saw Eduardo lying there so peacefully, as if he had simply gone to sleep, half on and half off the curb (but the
asphalt was so hot!). Then he noticed a thin stream of blood
running from Eduardo's nostrils and that his head was at a
funny angle. But his son was going to be all right, as soon as
he picked him up in his arms and carried him home. The
men from the ambulance that had just arrived would not let
him touch his boy, though, and they took charge of him with
firm and dexterous hands. As they were putting the boy on
the stretcher into the ambulance, Olga and Gloria arrived,
driven by Virginia, Al's sister.

"Where are you taking him?" Olga asked the ambulance
driver, her voice harsh and dry. Virginia then said that she
would drive them all to the hospital, and Mike said that he

would drop the car at their house. There seemed to be a conspiracy to keep him from driving his car. He remembered how white Olga's face was and how stiffly she held herself. In the back seat Gloria was crying soundlessly, tears coursing down her cheeks, as though independent from her. He had his hands clenched in his pockets, trying to stop the shaking. Virginia concentrated on driving and said nothing. No one said anything.

It was so cold in the hospital, so cold and bright in the emergency room waiting area. Inside, where people were working on his son, it must have been even colder. They had cut the clothes away from him. Eduardo looked so cold, so pale, lying there so still and naked. When they had finished with him and they brought him back out Eduardo's eyes were still closed. There was only a narrow bandage around his head, a bruise under one eye, a scraped elbow, to show that he was not merely sleeping. They wheeled him to a bed in the intensive care unit, and a young doctor then came to them. He explained that there were head injuries, internal bleeding, most likely, as well as the cut on the scalp, which, by itself was not serious. There could be a hemorrhage; there could be permanent brain damage. They would wait and observe him for the next few hours to determine which course to take. They could see him for a few minutes now; yes, they could touch him, but only very gently, and to stay only for a minute or so. And they had filed in by two's, he and Olga first, and later Gloria and Virginia.

Olga had touched the boy's quiescent hand and then placed her lips very lightly on it; she had also touched her fingers to her lips and then placed them on his cheek, where the bruise was. All that Al could do was stroke the boy's hand.

The long summer evening had become night, and they were still waiting. At some point Virginia had said that they all needed to eat. She left and after a while returned with styrofoam cups of coffee and sandwiches from the hospital cafeteria. Al did not want the sandwich, but ate half of it to please Virginia.

Virginia was older than he by four years, and the role of older sister reasserted itself now, as if they were all children once again. There had been a younger sister who had died in infancy of polio. Her name had been Gloria. When his first child was born, he had named her Gloria, as well. The name was not very popular now; it had an almost old fashioned ring about it, but he liked it.

Gloria had been an only child for eight years, and when his son was about to arrive, he prepared himself against disappointment. He loved his daughter; he would love another one just as much. But it was a boy, and not until the boy's birth had he realized how much he had wanted a son. Olga had expected to name the boy Al, Jr.—Al, for Alvaro—but he had said no. He had had enough of people mispronouncing his name. Why couldn't Anglos realize that the stress on *Alvaro* fell on the first syllable, just as in *Albert*. If they would only pay attention to how he said it, they could say it right, too. He disliked nicknames, but he had settled on Al, rather than have the mispronunciation grate against his ear constantly.

He was named Alvaro, after his grandfather on his mother's side, but he would call his son Eduardo. Not Ed and not Eddie. Even Anglos could not do too much to mispronounce Eduardo. Later, when the boy grew up, he could be Edward, if he wanted to, but, in the meantime, he would be Eduardo. Actually, he was Eduardito to Olga and to his grandmother when he was a baby, but after the grandmother died and the baby became a boy, even his mother called him Eduardo.

Once, during that long night, he was stricken with remorse, thinking what Olga must be going through and wondering whether it was true that the mother's grief was always the greatest. He could not imagine anyone's grief being greater than his own; it was already immense and took up every atom of his world. He had turned to look at his wife then and found, to his surprise, that she had a rosary in her hands and that she was fingering the beads as her lips moved without sound. She must have been carrying it in her handbag all this time, and he had known nothing about it.

Al and Olga went in once again to see the boy during the night, tiptoeing so as not to disturb the other patients in the unit. As they stood by his bed, one at each side like helpless guardian angels, Eduardo opened his eyes. They saw his eyelids flutter suddenly, and then, for perhaps less than a minute, his eyes were open and focused on some point floating over the bed. The two of them leaned forward, to get within his line of vision, holding their breath. Then Olga was whispering, "Eduardito, my baby, we are here with you."

Al took up her litany next, in Spanish, trying to make sure that he understood, "Eduardo, *hijo, m'hijo. . .*" That was all he could say, repeating the incantation, "my son, my son." The boy's eyes closed then, and he sighed, as if he were very tired. The nurse came at that moment and motioned them to leave the room.

While the wall clock ticked away the minutes inexorably, Al remembered noticing the small cacti plants in clay pots on a metal bookcase in one corner of the waiting area. He wondered what the cacti thought of the round-the-clock artificial light. No time for sleeping under that never-dimming white light. Gloria and Virginia, though, were huddled against the arms of the sofa, one at each end, sleeping softly. Olga recited the rosary for the fifth or tenth time, and he, himself, put his head down, between his arms, and hunched over thus, actually dozed off. He could not have slept more than ten or fifteen minutes, but he was ashamed of himself for having done so, wondering if his wife had noticed and if she had broken her vigil at all, or if she, alone, had watched without respite.

When the black sky outside lightened to pale gray, he stood up and stretched his legs by walking back and forth to the end of the hall and looked out the window as the street lights below him were extinguished at the same time as the stars, their counterparts above. With daybreak came a sudden scurrying of feet that woke Virginia and Gloria. The nursing shift change, he imagined. Virginia went off to the bathroom and then to the public telephone. He knew that she had called Joe, her husband, the night before, and Joe, no doubt, had called others: probably Al's cousin, Ray Medrano, and Olga's cousin, Marilu, as well, the next-door neighbors, if Mike had not already talked to them, and Minnie, his cashier at the pharmacy. Minnie had extra keys and would probably open the pharmacy this morning, but, just in case, Virginia was calling Joe again for him to remind Minnie.

Al thought that he had become numb with pain, that he felt all the pain that he would feel, but he was wrong. When a doctor, perhaps the same one as last night (he was past noticing), came to say that there must be emergency surgery, he reeled like a man receiving a blow. He signed the consent form and wanted to scream as they wheeled his boy down the corridor and into an elevator. He wanted to run after him, throw his arms around him, but the doors closed, and his child was gone.

Joe arrived with coffee and fresh *pan dulce*, the sweet yeast bread that he had always liked, but which tasted like chalk to him now. Joe said that he had talked to Minnie and that Al was not to worry about the pharmacy. Minnie would open and close up and had already gotten the young Camacho boy, who had just finished his pharmacy exams, to fill in for him behind the counter. Father Montalvo was saying prayers for Eduardito's recovery during today's Mass and would come by later in the morning. The Mendozas from next door were keeping an eye on the house.

Al looked dumbly at Joe and felt anger welling up inside him. He wanted to say, "You've thought of everything. You have all arranged everything. Why didn't you arrange to keep my boy safe?" But the effort to talk was as great as what was required to swallow the coffee and the bread, and he could not be bothered to do either. Instead, all his energies were focused on making a bargain with God, or with the devil, or whomever was now engaged in the struggle for his son's life. Months later, when he thought back on this hour, he could at least be glad of one thing: that not once had he offered his older child in exchange for his son. He had told God, over and over, "Take me, take me in his place."

But the Deity would not be fobbed off with a substitute, would not be cheated out of His chosen one. At noon, when the sun outside the windows put the pale, white light indoors to flight, they had told Al and Olga that it was all over. The boy's brain was dead, had been dead for some time; Al did not hear how long. The room spun in gray pirouettes around him. He thought that Olga and Gloria were in each other's arms, but all he could do was ask, "When did he die? When did he die, the exact moment? Why was I not told the exact moment it happened?" He did not know if he had actually said it aloud or had just thought it. He thought how he should have been by his son's side on the exact moment when his soul had flown out of him. He should have felt it, should have sensed the flight of the soul, and now it was gone, and he had not said goodbye.

How could they leave Eduardo behind, just because he was dead, for others to take charge of him? Al insisted on seeing him. He and Olga and Gloria filed past the bed in the screened off partition. They kissed the cheek that was now smooth and dry as parchment. And then they were gone, leaving behind the empty shell for others to do with as they would.

Al's house was not his anymore. It was filled with the voices of others, the gestures of others. Their neighbors were there, Nick and Lydia Mendoza, Tito and Nina Flores, who had been the first to reach the stricken boy, Joe and Virginia, his cousin Ray, Olga's cousin Marilu and their respective spouses, Father loose Montalvo, who was arranging for the funeral Mass, Gloria's best friend from high school . . . he lost track of them. And there were the telephone calls: Olga's family from the Valley, who would be coming up that evening, two or three of her fellow teachers and René Moreno, his friend from high school who went on to become a doctor and not just a pharmacist, as he had. René had seen them all through colds and flus and stomach viruses and had stitched up Eduardo's cut lip when he fell from the playground swing, but this time the problem was beyond what a simple doctor could remedy. No one was able to help—not the neurosurgeon, not God, Himself. Especially not God, Who willed it all, according to Father Montalvo, who seemed to know what was going on in heaven.

Al felt very cold and, strangely enough, also sleepy. He just wanted to leave them all talking in the living room, wanted to leave them with their covered casseroles in the kitchen, and close the bedroom door and go to sleep. Someone must have noticed him and his odd behavior because, soon after, René came by and, after murmuring condolences to him and Olga, some pills were left for them to take. He was not feeling bad, he told René; he just wanted to go to sleep. René nodded sagely and stood by while Al took one pill and then accompanied him to the bedroom. Just before Al closed the door behind him, he looked around for Olga. He had just one glimpse of her; her eyes were red and her face seemed to have crumpled, like a sheet of fine paper inside a fist, but he could hear her talking on the telephone about funeral arrangements. He shut the door and sat on the bed.

He did not remember lying down, but he woke up hours later, when the slanting rays of the evening sun came in through the slats of the blinds and filled the room with a rosy light. It was warm and still in the room, and he started to perspire under the afghan that someone had draped over him as he lay on his side with his knees drawn up. Someone must have turned down the air conditioner, he thought, as he pushed back the covers and sat up on the edge of the bed. He looked at the clock on the nightstand; it was 7:00. This time yesterday. . . . He got no further. Bile rose from his insides and came up his throat. He ran to the bathroom and was sick there.

When he was finished being sick, he washed his face and went into the living room. The house was quiet, the visitors had gone to let them rest, no doubt. He looked into Gloria's old room, which was now the spare room. His daughter and his wife were sleeping in a twin bed each. René's pills again, he thought. He felt hungry and went into the kitchen to find the refrigerator crowded with dishes brought by the visitors. There was even a bundle of tamales. Without much curiosity, he took a dish and it turned out to be a tuna and noodle casserole. He spooned some of it on a plate and warmed it in the microwave oven. It was a good thing that the food had absolutely no taste; otherwise he might not have been able to keep it down. When he finished, he left the plate in the sink, forgetting to rinse it out as Olga had taught him to do.

Al went into the dining room, which had the musty air of a room seldom used, and opened the sideboard where they kept three or four bottles of liquor, also seldom used. He took a bottle of scotch and carried it back to the kitchen, where he found a glass. He poured out a couple of jiggers into the glass and filled up the rest with water from the tap. Leaving the bottle on the counter, he went to the living room, where he turned on the television set. He flicked through various channels until he found a baseball game and, after turning down the sound, he sat down to watch the silent motions and gestures of the tiny men in uniforms and stared at the enlarged mouths and rolling eyes of men who drank beer and downed antacids between innings.

When he woke up, the house was in darkness, except for the blue light from the blank television screen. His glass was on the floor by the chair. He got up stiffly and switched off the set and, leaving the glass where it was, went back to bed, still in his clothes, and back to sleep again.

The following day the routine for coping with death asserted itself. There were still telephone calls, but now there was something that he could say to them. He could direct the callers to the rosary and the wake that evening at the funeral parlor and tell them at what time the funeral procession would leave for the requiem Mass the following morning and in which cemetery the interment would be.

Whereas the first day Al had wanted to do nothing but sleep, now he felt perfectly awake and without a desire to sleep again. He thanked the callers, feeling touched by their solicitude; he thanked their friends for their presence and for the beautiful flowers at the funeral. He felt remorseful for his earlier neglect of Olga and was shocked, on the day of the funeral, to see the naked sorrow on her face. She was the *mater dolorosa,* Our Lady of Sorrows from the Stations of the Cross on the stained glass windows at St. Joseph's Church. But still, she held herself in hand at the cemetery. Not a sound escaped her; only the tears that kept running down her face were beyond her control.

He had one arm around his wife, the other around Gloria, who sobbed softly against his shoulder as they stood by the graveside. He was the head of the family, the man of the house, the *pater familias,* comforting his womenfolk. Then it was back to the house, and once more came the covered dishes for the refrigerator. And after relatives and friends had left and after Gloria and Olga had dutifully taken their pills again and lay down once more (this time both of them in the queen-size bed in the master bedroom, at his own insistence), he tidied up the house late into the night. Then he sat down to organize the florists' cards and made a list of the thank-you notes to be sent out.

He let two days go by before returning to work. People expected it; they would have been a little shocked and probably embarrassed to see him behind the counter, waiting on them, so soon after the tragedy. When he returned, everyone was so kind; even casual customers stopped by to offer sympathy. Gratitude flowed from him to them.

Then the anger came. One day the questions could no longer be avoided. What had happened exactly? Who had killed his boy? What had happened to his killers? He called the police department and tracked down the officer who made the report. It had been a hit and run, the officer said, rather superfluously (he knew that), but the culprits were apprehended the following day, thanks to the witnesses at the scene. The officer gave him the remaining facts, as he knew them.

The story (the fateful chain of events, as he thought of it) began early that Saturday afternoon when the three young men, who were seventeen, sixteen and fourteen, had procured a bottle of bourbon somehow and began drinking in the park. There was also the possibility that they had been sniffing glue. At some point, they ran out of liquor and decided to obtain more. They tried to buy a six-pack at a convenience store off the freeway, but the clerk demanded identification and proof of age, and they left empty handed. The next attempt at obtaining alcohol was at the neighborhood Insta-mart. One of the boys, the sixteen-year-old, Donato, "Donny" Segura, lived nearby so, perhaps, that was why they chose this particular store.

At any rate (said the officer), while Segura shoplifted two six-packs of beer, he was observed by the salesclerk, who attempted to stop him. At that point the seventeen-year-old Mack López pushed the clerk out of the way, knocking him down to the ground, and all three ran out and jumped in the car that Segura was driving without a license. It was his mother's car, and he had taken the keys from her handbag without her knowledge, she claimed.

The boys drove away erratically and before going a block, had swerved to avoid an oncoming car and, in the process, brushed against Eduardo who was pedaling his bicycle close to the curb. It was just a glancing blow, but it knocked the bike over. Eduardo hit his head on the curb.

What was being done to those thugs, Al wanted to know. When were they coming to trial? "Well, as you know," the policeman explained, "Segura is still a juvenile. I really shouldn't have even mentioned his name. Juveniles' names are not released, as you know, but everybody in the store saw him and most of them know him. Not the fourteen-year-old; he's not a neighborhood boy. And López just moved in recently with his aunt and uncle, who live in the neighborhood."

What about bringing them to trial, he repeated the question. The juveniles had been detained by the juvenile authorities. The oldest boy was in jail on a charge of assault on the store clerk while prosecutors decided which would be the best charge to stick him with. The fourteen-year-old would probably be released from the juvenile facility to his parents since he seemed to have been merely going along for the ride, but the sixteen-year-old would stay in detention until disposition was made. He was not a good risk for release, did not seem to have a very stable home, just a mother who couldn't control him.

Al did not care what kind of home life the young thugs had; he just wanted them punished. His son had had a loving home; it had not saved him. Throughout the summer Al continued his calls to the police department (they eventually referred him to the crime victims' assistance group) and, later, to the prosecutor's office as well, where they told him that they were still investigating the case. Then it came out. The seventeen-year old's lawyer made a deal with the prosecutor. López had been facing a possible felony murder charge if the prosecutors could show that Eduardo's death had resulted from the same transaction as the assault and robbery. It was a tenuous connection, but threatening enough that López' attorney had come forth with an offer. His client had information about a burglary ring on the border. He would cooperate in exchange for immunity from the murder charge and a guilty plea to assault. The prosecutor took the bait. The sixteen-year-old was adjudicated a delinquent and had already been sent to a long-term youth detention facility. The fourteen-year-old had moved out of town, and there were no charges pending against him.

Al was stunned and outraged, his grief temporarily forgotten, and its place taken up by anger. Anger carried him through the summer and mobilized him into a frenzy of activity. He talked to Joe's cousin who worked for the sheriff's office. The cousin sent him to talk to a lawyer who, after two weeks of telephone calls to various assistant prosecutors, told him that there was nothing to be gained by further importuning prosecutors. The wheels of justice had ground to a halt, and the most that could be done had been done.

At this time his cousin Ray, had taken him aside and told him that, although everybody understood that he had suffered perhaps the greatest blow that a parent could receive, it was time that he took hold of himself before things got out of hand. Ray went on to point out that business at the pharmacy was bound to be affected from Al's lack of attention, but even more important, as a professional man, Al had to be particularly careful. A pharmacist had to be sure that he did not make a mistake. In addition, as a family man, he had to remember that his wife and child were also suffering.

Al looked at Ray with a dull hatred that precluded words (what did this man know about suffering?) but, if Ray noticed his cousin's anger, he gave no indication of it. Nevertheless, Al looked at his wife for the first time in weeks and was filled with shame at the sight of her pale, frozen face. In his grief he had forgotten her. Gloria wandered about, too, like a little frightened ghost in a house empty of living creatures. "Our daughter is afraid of us," was the startling thought he had. "She is afraid of her mother and of me—but why? Because she is alive, and her brother is dead, and she wonders if we wish that it was the other way around," the answer came to him with amazing detachment.

Gloria had moved back with them since that terrible weekend, but now, as summer vacation wound to an end, she timidly broached the idea that perhaps she needed to make plans to find a new apartment. Her old roommate, who was away with a summer job, was coming back to town, and she needed to let her know whether she would be sharing an apartment with her for the school year. He could not tell if the girl wanted to be asked to stay, or if it would be a relief for her to escape the glacial grief that encased her parents.

Al tried to strike a spark of warmth. He put his arm around her, called her his little girl, told her that he loved her and wanted to have her close to him always, but that she must not let her roommate down, that it was better for her to be like other college students and live with those of her own age group. She should enjoy her college years; they were among the best in life. He had really meant his answer to be altruistic, but, in truth, he wanted her to be gone. He wanted school to resume so his wife would go back to work as well and he would not have to feel responsible for the two women anymore. He wanted to be left alone.

Agnus Dei

By early September, Gloria moved out again, and Olga went back to teach her first graders. Now he could come home in the middle of the day, and, in the silence of the house, he could sense his son's presence again, even hear his footsteps very faintly. He had feared, early on, that Olga would want to clean out the boy's room, give away his clothes, and he had asked her not to change anything in it yet. He, himself, did not have the courage to go into the room at first, but now, when he was alone, he found solace in sitting in there, with his son's possessions around him.

Al would tell them at the pharmacy that he was going out for lunch to pick up a hamburger, which he would take home. After eating in the kitchen, he would clean up after himself, carefully washing out his plate and glass. He was not trying to keep Olga from learning that he had been in the house, but neither did he tell her or leave a trail for her to find when she came home. He would always be back at the pharmacy before Olga's classes let out.

Sometimes Al would go into the boy's room and sit in the rocking chair that was placed exactly in front of the window; sometimes he would lie in the narrow bed, carefully smoothing out the bedspread afterwards to erase the imprint of his body on the bed. Sometimes he would open the closet door and bury his face among the boy's clothes. He thought that the boy's scent still lingered over them, but one day he realized that Olga had been at work, because there was a fresh and overpowering odor of mothballs that had not been there before. He would pass his fingertips over the boy's combs and brushes that still held captive a silky hair or two from his head, pass his hands over the folded underclothes in the dresser drawers, gaze at the family portrait on the dresser, at the snapshots tucked into the mirror frame: Eduardito with his scouting group, Eduardito in his Little League uniform, Eduardito and friends at a picnic in the park. Then there were the posters of rock musicians on the walls and the school pennants on cork boards. The room was always ready to receive a twelve-year-old boy who would never grow old.

Another time he wondered what had happened to the

bicycle and burrowed frantically among the odds and ends that filled up the garage. He wanted to keep the bicycle and prayed that it had not been thrown out after the police had returned it. It was not in the garage, but he found it, by itself, in the utility room. There it stood, defeated and dejected, like a mythical steed that had borne the dead body of its rider, propped up against the wall, its rear-end wheel bent and dented and a helmet cradled in the basket that hung from the handlebars. There had been a question, at the time of the accident, of whether the boy had been wearing his helmet or if it had been fastened properly, but he refused to see the event in the light of simple accident prevention when it had the proportions of a cosmic tragedy. He left the bicycle where it was.

One afternoon he drove across town and watched Eduardo's classmates as they came out of school. He sat in the airless car that baked in the already lengthening but still hot October sun, parked half a block away from the entrance to the school, and saw the little ones come out first. Some were so young they were still downy, like chicks just out of the shell. He saw them scampering into waiting station wagons, driven by harassed looking women whose turn it was to car pool that week. He thought that the drivers looked at him suspiciously as they drove past him, but he did not care. Half an hour later the older ones, the sixth through eighth graders, came out, most of them making purposefully toward the white and maroon bus that waited at the curb, while the others dispersed along the neighboring streets. A wave of anguish washed over him as he noticed two or three boys that he knew had been Eduardo's classmates. There was already an air of grownup self-assurance about them that was not there last spring. They were already growing up away from his boy, who would remain twelve years old forevermore. He wanted to run after them, ask them if they still remembered their absent classmate, but he noticed a private security car driving slowly past him, the driver looking intently at him, as if trying to memorize his features. He wanted to tell the driver, "I have a right to be here. My son used to be a student

here. I just wanted to know if they still remembered him."
But he drove away instead and did not go back.

Eduardo's class had a memorial service for him at the
beginning of the semester, and both he and Olga attended,
but he had not been back to the school since then. He had
always felt uncomfortable visiting his son's school, but proud,
as well. His son attended private school, he would tell others,
a little defiantly, uncertain as to what his listener's reaction
would be. Sometimes he would see respect, mingled with
envy, in their eyes; sometimes hostility would harden like a
mask over the listeners' features.

Al himself, had gone, of course, to public schools in his
neighborhood, his *barrio*. They had been old, neglected structures filled with a sea of faces that ranged from chocolate to
cream. The teachers, on the other hand, were almost all Anglos and ranged from cruel to indifferent to heroic. It was
almost a miracle that he and a handful of his classmates were
admitted to college after graduation from such schools and an
even greater miracle that they managed to graduate from college and even receive professional degrees, due mainly to
their own determination to succeed and to the few heroic
teachers.

When he returned from college, with a wife who was a
school teacher, he went to work at the Midtown Pharmacy.
Olga began teaching at his old elementary school (fortunately
now housed in a new building), where Mexican teachers were
now in the majority. She took off a couple of years from work
after Gloria was born, but when Gloria was ready to start
school, what better arrangement than for her to attend school
where her mother was already teaching? So mother and
daughter went off to school together for six years.

Schools change, though, and so do the kinds of children in
them. By the time that Eduardito started the third grade,
Olga had to admit that the neighborhood schools did not offer
the levels of courses that a child as bright as Eduardito
should have. In addition, the children in her grade and her
colleagues' had problems and experiences that she and Al
wanted to keep from their son. There were physically abused

children; children who spoke of home experiences involving drugs and crime as if they were everyday occurrences. Al and Olga decided to enroll Eduardo in a private school to avoid the problems and the limitations of their neighborhood schools.

Al had been apprehensive about taking his child across town and leaving him among strangers who might slight him on account of where he lived, on account of who he was, on account of being named Eduardo Estrada. Besides, there was something snooty about private schools. Catholic schools might be all right. Sometimes their tuition was so low that they might as well have been free, and naturally, many Mexican children were enrolled in them. But Eduardo's school was run by Protestants, and they were all Anglos, of course.

Eduardito had done very well there, though. He had had a natural grace that precluded him from being either self-conscious or defensive about the fact that he lived in the old part of town that had become, as far back as fifty years ago, the Mexican *barrio*. Eduardo was a bright child—not a child prodigy—but one to whom learning was a joy. He made good grades, he loved sports and games, and he formed new friendships in school without forgetting his old friends from the neighborhood.

On that fateful Saturday, Olga took the boy to meet a school friend who had invited him to go swimming at a private club. Those were the kinds of friends that he had made at school, Al thought proudly: children whose parents belonged to private clubs with swimming pools and tennis courts. But then Al felt a little embarrassed by his pride—or was it snobbery?

Olga had dropped Eduardo off at the club on her way to the mall and asked him at what time she should pick him up, but the boy, on his way to being a young man, asserted his independence and insisted that he would get home on his own. He would ride the bus across town and pick up the bicycle that he had left with his father at the pharmacy and go home from there. Olga gave in to his determination, but she called Al from the mall to tell him about Eduardo's plans.

It was that crosstown bus ride that worried Al, although the worry was followed by a feeling of pride at his son's independence. His boy was no pampered sissy; he had as much street smarts as any kid from the neighborhood. Nevertheless, before Al left the pharmacy to get his hair cut, he asked Minnie to have Eduardo call him at the barber shop when he turned up, and the boy did so. "And that was the last time I heard his voice!" The cry was torn from him like a howl of pure anguish. The boy made it across town safely; he returned safely to the bosom of his people, of his neighborhood. "And here was where the danger lay . . . and how little we knew it!"

That was the thought that now tormented him. He had exhausted the questions, importuned the heavenly and the earthly powers for an answer: Why had it happened? Why to him? Why to his beautiful boy? Why had a wonderful, intelligent boy been taken, one who held such promise, when the wastrels and the delinquents were left to thrive? Was it something that *he* had done wrong? He had loved his child; he had cared for his body and for his spirit and still had lost him. And those who neglected their children, who actually hurt them, still had them. It did not make sense. He *must* have done something wrong, but his sin must be so enormous that at first it would not be apparent. It was apparent to him now.

Al remembered how lonely he was when he first went away to study at the university. He was poor and had to work at various part-time jobs to pay for his room and board at school. The money for his tuition and books, though, came from a neighborhood civic club scholarship. He was so grateful to the members of the club—men who were his father's friends and contemporaries, all working men—for making it possible for him to go to college that he promised himself, that when he graduated, he would go back to that same neighborhood and join people like those who had raised money for his scholarship. He would help others coming after him.

The thought of those people back home, wishing him well, helping him get his education, was the hearth at which he had warmed himself from a distance to offset the coldness of students and professors at the university. At the university they were all indifferent to his success or failure. It did not matter at the great university whether he stayed or went, but it mattered back home.

Then he met some students from the Rio Grande Valley, from the southmost part of the state. They were Mexicans, like him, a tiny number in that sea of pale faces and pale eyes. They had an informal group that got together to study and to party, that shared rides home during the holidays and came back with bottles of rum from Mexico and homemade goodies, like flour tortillas, which were still unknown then in the university town. Al did not properly belong with them in that he was not from the Valley, but he was a Mexican, and so they adopted him. They admitted him to their circle of warmth, and his life became much happier after that.

Olga was part of that group. He was drawn to her from the first. She was attractive without being beautiful, with a smile that brightened up her whole face, and a sensible, level-headed disposition that balanced his more mercurial temperament. They were soon a couple. She was an elementary education major and finished her degree while he still had a year left in his pharmacy program. He panicked at the thought that she would leave town after graduating and take a job back home in the Valley. She might forget him there. Three hundred miles was a long way for frequent visits. He asked her to marry him then, and she agreed, and they had a late summer wedding in her hometown.

That first year of their marriage, Olga got a teaching job in the school where she had done her student teaching while he finished his degree. Only when he received his own degree and passed his state board exams had he told her that his plans had always been to go back home to work among his neighbors. He was apprehensive that Olga might insist on moving back to her hometown, where she had *her* friends and family, or might even want to stay where she was since she enjoyed her job. But she accepted and supported his ideals and even looked forward to the move.

Al knew that Mr. Inks, owner and dispensing pharmacist of Midtown Pharmacy, was getting close to retirement age and was looking for a younger person to take over much of the daily work from him. Al talked to Mr. Inks, who first hired him as a relief pharmacist. Inks knew Al since he was a boy and employed him at his pharmacy as part-time clerk while Al was in high school. Inks was a good man, but Al always wondered why Anglos and Jews would set up businesses in the barrio and never live among the people they traded with.

Al decided to have his own business someday and to continue living among the people he worked with not like his cousin Ray. That was the way his grandfather had done it. His grandfather Alvaro Medrano, for whom he had been named, had a small grocery and meat market. Conrado his son—Ray's father and Al's uncle—had inherited it. Medrano's Meat Market survived for over fifty years at the same location in the middle of the neighborhood. When the store had come down to Ray, he sold it to a chain of convenience stores, the Instamarts in the name of progress and efficient money management.

Perhaps there was divine irony in there . . . somewhere. Ray had sold out and moved away, to a new subdivision with proper zoning controls and homogenized, sanitized development that insured well-ordered lives. Al, on the other hand, had gone to the bank and to the Small Business Administration and gotten a loan with which to buy out Mr. Inks, replacing the "Midtown Pharmacy" sign with a new one that read "Al's Pharmacy." He threw in his lot with the future of the neighborhood. And look what had happened—to him, to his son, to his entire family!

That was his sin. Al had sacrificed his son to an imaginary cause. He could have owned and run the pharmacy in the barrio, but he did not have to live there. Mr. Inks had not done so. Al could have gone to work for a large pharmaceutical chain, with a good salary and benefits, instead of worrying about meeting a payroll, about drug addicts holding up the store, and about pilfering shortages. If he had lived in a new subdivision, like Ray's, his child would have walked the streets in safety and could have attended public schools that were as good as private schools, without having to strain to pay high tuition. His wife could have worked in a new school building without graffiti on the walls and with happy, healthy children.

What had he achieved by his gesture—the gesture of living in the same house he had grown up in, the gesture of sending his children to the schools he had attended? For it was only a gesture, one made for his own satisfaction, that of telling the long-dead members of the sociedad mutualista that had sent him to college, "See, I have repaid your trust and generosity tenfold. I kept your ideals. I lived them. I did this for you and for my people."

These thoughts brought to his mind a story from the Bible that he had read when he was still a member of the Catholic Youth Organization and took religion seriously. It was a story that he had never fully understood: the story of Abraham and Isaac. Abraham and his wife had grown old without having children, and they prayed to God for a child, and God finally answered their prayers. Since God could do everything, a son was born to Sarah, Abraham's wife, although she was past childbearing age. Abraham and Sarah named their son Isaac, and he was their pride and joy.

Then, one day, when Isaac was a young boy, God told Abraham that he wanted him to sacrifice his son to Him. In those days people used to sacrifice their best crops, or their best lambs, if they were shepherds, to honor and give thanks to God. But with Abraham, God was not satisfied with a lamb. He wanted Abraham's only child. Abraham had been devastated by God's request (did God ever "request" or was it a command?). Abraham wondered if he dared to disobey God and was torn between his love of God and his love for his son.

Abraham finally decided to obey God's command, and he set about, with a heavy heart, to build the altar on which he would sacrifice his son to God's will. God intervened at the last minute, though, and spared Isaac. He had just been testing Abraham's love and obedience. He did not really want that ultimate sacrifice.

"But He wanted mine," was his silent scream. "Why did He not intervene to save my son, even if it was at the last minute?"

He could not understand God making such a demand of anyone. But perhaps it had not been God who had asked for his sacrifice. It seemed clear to him now that he, himself, had offered up his son as sacrifice in the name of an idea, of a false god. Lambs were once offered as sacrifice; that was why Isaac would have been the Lamb of God. That is why, during the Mass, you prayed to Christ, the Lamb of God, who had offered Himself as sacrifice to take away the sins of the world. And Al, poor mortal, had sacrificed his own lamb, his only son—but not to God.

Olga must realize this. Olga must know it, and she must blame him for taking away her son. (How did Sarah feel when Abraham led Isaac to the altar?) That was why Olga avoided looking at him, avoided being alone with him.

Al was seized then with the thought of the aging Abraham and Sarah bringing forth a child. Olga was twenty-four when Gloria was born and thirty-two when Eduardo finally arrived. Gloria was twenty now; Olga was forty-four and he, himself, forty-five. Perhaps they could still have another child. And he had turned to his wife in blind anguish during the night and had clung to her. Perhaps she realized that the embrace was not for her, but for the child that he wanted to reengender because, although she accepted him, she still remained in a space of her own where he could not reach her.

Afterwards, Al felt angry and ashamed of himself. His wife would have good reason to reject him. It was not she that he had wanted. Nor was it a child not yet conceived. He wanted his son, Eduardo. He wanted his beautiful boy with the smooth torso, already elongating towards manhood, and the golden down on the slender legs not yet touched by puberty. He wanted the actuality of his son at twelve and the promise of him at twenty—Eduardo, who was a joyful child and who would have been a doctor or a scientist or anything wonderful as an adult. He wanted the children that would have come from Eduardo and the comfort they would have brought him in his old age. All that was dead, and he had killed it at an altar of his own making.

One afternoon he stayed too long in the boy's room, or perhaps Olga came home early. He was still sitting in the rocking chair, holding a geography book, Eduardo's sixth-grade textbook. Olga did not seem surprised to find him there. Maybe she had guessed already that he spent time there often. She hesitated at the door and asked, "May I come in?" as if she were a guest in her own son's room. Al nodded, relieved that his secret was out. Olga sat down on the edge of the bed. They sat in silence for some time, and then she said, without preamble, "Not a day goes by that I do not hate myself for not having picked him up at the swimming pool and brought him home with me."

He looked at her in astonishment, trying to think of how to tell her that she had it all wrong.

She continued, before he had a chance to say anything, "If I had not been so insistent on having a career, I would have been the kind of mother, like his classmates have, the kind that stays at home and carpools and drives her children everywhere. Those children don't take buses across town or go places on bicycles. Their mothers *drive* those children everywhere."

He was out of the chair and sitting next to her on the bed in one motion. He took her hand. "But it was Saturday, and it was summer vacation . . . so you were home, anyway. That did not make any difference. And just think, think of that poor woman the other day, the one who had the accident on the freeway, her little girl was in the car with her and got killed. She must feel that she is to blame, and, yet, she could not have avoided it; some other car hit her."

They sat in silence again, and he wondered whether he should tell her the truth: that he, alone, was to blame for bringing them to live in a place where violence—from accidents, from crimes—was so much a part of a person's life it bred in every one of them a kind of reckless fatalism that actually courted tragedy. Had he convinced her that she was not to blame? Should he confess his guilt to her, and in confessing to her, would he receive absolution? But before he could speak again, she began to weep softly and, taking her hand away from his, covered her face with it. He put his arm around her shoulders and pulled her towards him so that she now wept against his chest in great racking sobs.

For the first time since his son's death, Al felt that he had a responsibility for others, not only the self-imposed mission of seeking justice for his dead son or of finding the reason for what had happened, but a responsibility to the living, to his wife and to his daughter. Olga stopped sobbing finally, and he found a clean handkerchief in the boy's dresser drawer and gave it to her. She hesitated before using it, but then covered her face with it.

When Olga had dried her eyes, she turned her tear-streaked face to him and said huskily, "Do you know the only thing that has made this loss, this horrible, terrible loss bearable? That I have not been alone. That we have not been alone. We have the comfort of our families, our friends, our neighbors. Can you imagine—if Eduardito had had the accident somewhere else, at that swimming pool, for example— can you imagine what it would have been like for him to be hurt among strangers? How long would it have taken for anyone to notify us? To find us? And for us to have reached him? If we lived in one of those subdivisions, like the one Ray and Mary live in, where nobody knows their neighbors, who would have comforted him until we got there? As it was, the . . . the accident . . . happened in front of Nina Flores' house, and while Tito called the ambulance, she sent young Art to find you at the pharmacy, and when you weren't there, he ran to the barber shop to tell you while she put a blanket over my baby and kept him warm and talked to him so he wouldn't be afraid, even though he probably could not hear what she said. And then she called me because she knew that I was with Virginia. If we had not known our neighbors, if it had happened somewhere else, my baby would have been lying alone in the street. We might not have even been at the hospital with him, those moments when he opened his eyes and saw us. I know he saw us, and it made a difference to him to know that we were there.

"And afterwards, how could we have coped, without friends or neighbors? Everyone has been so good, so kind since then. The club is even going to raise funds for a scholarship in Eduardito's name so that he will not be forgotten."

She looked at him through eyes that were bright with tears and with gratitude. His own eyes overflowed, and he buried his face in her hair to hide them. "Thank you," he prayed silently. When he least expected it, when he had given up hope, it had happened. It was perhaps a miracle. It was perhaps—absolution.

Pilgrimage

I

"Do you see that turtledove up in that tree? On the dead branch? Do you suppose she really is in mourning . . . for her mate, I mean?"

"What—?"

"You have never heard that? About turtledoves not perching on a green branch when they have lost their mates? I think it is true. I noticed that dove before. Did you say something?"

"Nothing—I just wanted to ask—is this where I catch the number 37 bus?"

"That's right. That's what it says up there."

"Do you know if that bus has already gone by?"

"About ten minutes ago. There will be another one in about twenty minutes. Where do you want to go?"

"Ah . . . Market Street."

"Market is a long street. Where on Market?"

"The big shopping center. The one with the tower in the middle."

"You are going to the mall . . . shopping? Or do you work around there? That's all right, you don't have to tell me if you don't want to."

"It isn't that . . . I'm sorry. . ."

"You didn't hurt my feelings. I know that sometimes I meddle in what is not my business. That's the way I am . . . curious. But look how rude I am too. Here I am, eating these doughnuts and not offering you any. Would you like one?"

"No, thank you. I already had breakfast."

"Well, so did I. When a person works hard, like I do, and, I imagine you do too—well, one needs a good breakfast. But I like to get these doughnuts to have afterwards. For dessert, you know. Come on, have one at least. Which kind would you like?"

"Thank you, since you insist. I will have one with chocolate on top. They look very appetizing."

"They are fresh. I get them at that stand over there, on the corner. I like to come early and get some pastry and sit here to eat it while I wait for the bus. I catch number 37 too, but I transfer before I get to the shopping center so I will not be able to help you if you have a question about how to get to where you are going. Maybe the driver can help you, if you ask him. Sometimes you get one that speaks Spanish."

"It's all right. I know how to get there once I see the tower."

"You know how to get . . . where? . . . Never mind. By the way, I have not introduced myself. My name is Odilia González. Forgive me if I do not shake hands with you, but I have chocolate on my fingers."

"Very happy to meet you. My name is Modesta. Modesta Camacho de Rodríguez, at your service."

"Ah, you are married. Does your husband live here too? Forgive me again. Would you like another doughnut? No? Are you sure? I am going to have just one more. You see how skinny I am? I have always been thin, and I eat more than most people. That's just the way I am. But I am always very active, never still. The ladies that I work for are surprised at how fast I finish my work. Do you have any children?"

"Yes, three—I mean, two. One died . . ."

"How sad! How very sad when a child dies! I am not married, but I have always heard that a woman suffers much more when she loses a child than if she loses her husband. That must be so. Are the children here with you? No? How sad for you. I don't mean to pry, but I can tell that you are new here. Now, I have lived in this town for over ten years, closer to fifteen. It was hard at first. I lived then with my cousin, but after I had been working for some time I moved to a little apartment of my own. I tell you, I was scared at first living alone, but I have good neighbors, and I like my independence. I like having my things just so, and with my cousin I had to sleep on the sofa in the living room, and I didn't even have a place to hang up my clothes. I looked after her children at first, but of course, she didn't pay me, just room and board—and not much room at that. Not that I am ungrateful, you know. I always appreciate whatever people do for me, and I appreciate what my cousin did to help me. She is the one who got me across."

"Really? How did she do that?"

"It was after my mother died. I was an only child, and my mother had been a widow for many years. My parents married late, and my father died when I was ten. My mother had a little store where she sold soft drinks, candy, chewing gum, some newspapers—that sort of thing—and she supported both of us that way. We lived in the back and had the store in the front room. I helped her in the store ever since I learned how to count and make change. Ever since my father retired from the railroads, my mother ran the store. The pensions are pitiful. A cat could not live on them. Anyway, after my father died, I wanted to stay home and help my mother. But she said, no, I had to finish my primary school. And I did. But after that, I helped my mother in the store, and then, when I was older, I went to work for a man who had a shoe-repair shop. He was paralyzed from the waist down, and all he could do was to sit, surrounded by shoes, as he resoled them and put on new heels. He needed someone to work the counter, to take in the shoes and write the names of the owners on the ticket and take payment for the repairs. I liked that; there were so many people always coming and going. I made so many friends there. I was there for years, but then my mother got sick, and I had to be close to her, so I took over the little store and looked after her. When she died, I was so lonely! The neighbors were all very kind, but I had no brothers or sisters or relatives, except some distant relations of my father that I never got along with. All my close relatives—cousins—lived far away. My cousin Irma, who lived in the

United States, came to visit me and said, 'You are all alone now, you have no responsibilities to anyone, why don't you come and stay with me for some time?'"

"And did you accept?"

"Well, you know, it meant closing down the store, but I thought, 'Why not?' and so I sold off the inventory—but kept the shelves and the counter, just in case I wanted to go back. I packed my clothes—I was ready for a change. I had no boyfriend or husband or anyone to make demands on me, so I did not have to consult anyone to make my decision, but, just to be sure that I was doing the right thing, I went and talked to the priest. My mother had always trusted him. I am not very religious, but I keep the Church's commandments as best as I can. Father Ordóñez, he was a good man, said, 'If your cousin is giving you this opportunity to see what another country is like, there is no reason why you should not take it. God will take care of you if you lead a good, decent life anywhere.' So, as I said, I packed my clothes and said goodbye to my friends. Then we drove to the border with my cousin and her husband and their three children. My cousin Irma, asked the American immigration official for a tourist visa for me and told them that I was going to stay with them for a few weeks, and they gave it to me."

"Your cousin's name is Irma? I have a sister named Irma, and she married a man who repairs shoes."

"Really? What a coincidence. Where did you say you were from?"

"I just arrived here from California. I lived in Burbank."

"California? Really? I would not have thought . . . Well, anyway, do you like it here?"

"I think so, but it is very hot, especially because of the humidity."

"And what does your husband think? I forget, did you say that he was not with you? No? But you must live in the neighborhood—who do you live with? Forgive me for meddling in what is not my business, but you are still young, and you have to be careful."

"Yes, I know, but I am staying with an older lady. Very

respectable. She is the aunt of a . . . friend of mine."

"Here comes the bus. Let's see if we can find seats together. . . . How fortunate, we will be able to sit together until I get off. Well, I will tell you something: I will not deny that when you said that you had come from California I was surprised. You don't look like it. Please do not be offended, but there is a certain look . . . There are some, poor things, who look like they just came down from the hills, and they get picked up in no time at all. Your hair is too long. You need to have it cut, shaped well, you know, and wear some color on your lips, too. Not too much, of course, because you are still young, and there are some men that are just looking for women who are alone. Your children are not with you, are they? Where are they?"

"With my mother . . ."

"Oh, then they are probably well cared for. And where are they?"

"In my mother's home."

"Yes?"

"In Zacatacas."

"How many are there? You said two? Boys or girls? What are their names?"

"Two little girls. Carmelita is nine by now, and Maricela is gong to be five."

"And the one that died? Was it in infancy?"

"He would be seven now. Juanito. Juan Mario. I named him after my husband and my brother. He died when he was three."

"Poor little angel. And was your husband very sad when his only son died? Where is your husband now, do you know?"

"No . . . I . . . they told me he was dead."

"They *told* you he was dead! Don't you know? ¡*Válgame Dios*! Here is my stop . . . I must get out here. Goodbye, take care of yourself."

‖

"Good morning. . . . We met here the other day. . . ."

"Oh, yes, of course. I remember now. Modesta, Modesta Camacho—right?"

"I had not seen you again . . ."

"That's because I only catch this bus on Tuesdays and Thursdays. That was last Thursday that I saw you, wasn't it?"

"I was thinking of something that you said the other day. I hope you will forgive me if I ask you a question . . ."

"What is it?"

"You said that when you came across you got a tourist visa, and I was wondering how you get one. I have found a regular job here and . . ."

"Yes, but you cannot work on a tourist visa. This is the way it was: At first I came just to visit my cousin, to have a change of air, you know, after my mother died. And at first I was just staying at home, looking after her children, just as a favor, while my cousin and her husband were at work. Well, when the children's summer vacation was over, and they went back to school, what was there for me to do? There I was, stuck in the house, watching all those television shows where they have contests and give away prizes—in English, which I did not understand, because at that time my cousin's TV did not get the Spanish stations. I am not used to being idle, so I asked my cousin if she knew of any opportunities where I could work a little. I wanted to earn some money; I could not go on being another hungry mouth for them to feed. Nothing permanent, you know, because I thought that I would be going back to my home very soon. I think that my cousin was a little embarrassed, but relieved, too, I think, that I would not be a burden on them. Anyway, she said that she would look around and then, later, told me that the only thing that she knew about was helping out this woman to clean her house. Well, I had never been a servant for anybody, but I thought, Why not? It is all different in this country, and, anyway, nobody knows me here. No one back home will ever hear about it. So I began cleaning houses ever so often, and I was good at it. I am good at doing whatever I set out to do, but then my cousin got me worried, saying that I was not supposed to be working because of the tourist visa, and the visa was about to run out, too."

"So what did you do?"

"We went down to the border and got an extension on the visa, but this time the immigration people were very rude and did not want to give me the extension. They finally said they would give me one more extension, but that was all. I had to leave the country after that. When we returned from the border, I was feeling very bad. I told my cousin that the immigration man had made me feel like a criminal, and that maybe I would just go back home. I did not want to stay where I was not wanted. But then my cousin told me that her boss had asked her for a favor. She needed her help in finding someone—a responsible, mature woman, she said—to take care of her, the boss's mother. She was an old lady who had had a cerebral hemorrhage and was paralyzed. Have you ever seen someone like that? She could not move her left arm or leg and could not speak. I asked what about the language problem? How was the old lady going to communicate with me or I with her, but they said, don't worry, she can't talk, anyway. By this time I understood some English, though. I could read many of the signs on the streets and understand words that I had learned from the TV shows. I met with my cousin's boss, and the woman said that if I took care of her mother and if they were happy with me, they would get me my permanent resident card, the green card. So I agreed to work there, taking care of the old lady. I had to live in her house. It was a nice house, old fashioned, but you could tell that the things she had were good, and with all the modern conveniences, like a washing machine and a dishwasher. I had to bathe the old lady every day and change her—she wore diapers—and turn her in bed so that she did not get bedsores. It was not that different from caring for my mother, so I already knew what to do. I also gave her her medicine. I had to be on duty twenty-four hours a day, but of course, the old lady slept a great deal and left me time to watch television and for knitting and reading and keeping the house clean. I had my own room, right next to the old lady's room. I always slept with the door open to her room so that I could hear if she had any problems. At first I fed her by mouth, but then she got worse, and they put a tube down her throat. I had to feed her that way too, being very careful that everything was clean and that she did not choke on the liquid. I did a good job for them, twenty-four hours a day, with only Sundays off. Nobody else wanted work like that, not just one person for doing everything and not earning very much, but they got me my green card, and I stayed with them. That was the agreement that we had made. I stayed until the old lady got very bad, and they had to put her in the hospital. She died soon after that, and they gave me a big Christmas bonus when I left."

"What did you do then, when you were without a job?"

"I had no trouble at all getting another job, now that I did not have to worry about the immigration men coming to pick me up. First, I went to work for this doctor's family. As a matter of fact, he was a friend of the old lady's doctor. They had a big house and two children, and I had my own rooms, a bedroom and a bathroom over the garage, with my own television set, all air conditioned. Before I went to work for the doctor though, I went back home and sold my house and the shelves and counter from the store. I had decided that I would probably stay here, and there was no sense in having the house shut up. The neighbors had looked after it, but it was only a matter of time until hoodlums started breaking windows and stealing my things."

"What did you do in that doctor's house?"

"I was a housekeeper for the doctor's family. I even learned to cook fancy dishes for them, and I kept the whole house clean. I liked the two children; they were about ten or twelve then. They were nice to me, but it was shocking to see how disrespectful they were to their parents. Then they got a dog. I have never liked dogs, but this one was not very big, and I thought maybe I could get used to it. What I could not get used to was cleaning up the dog's messes. I drew the line at that: it was either the dog or me. They seemed very put out with my attitude—so I left.

"I went to work for another doctor and his wife. They were older—the couple, and the children. They had two daughters. Then the daughters went away to study, and by this time I was getting tired of living in other people's houses, even with my own room. It was just as if I was on duty twenty-four hours a day. I told the lady that I would work for her every day from eight in the morning until five in the afternoon, like in an office. She didn't like that, but she knew that she would have a hard time finding someone dependable and honest like me. That's when I got my own little apartment. I still work for that lady, but only three times a week—Mondays, Wednesdays and Fridays—and for another family on Tuesdays and Thursdays. On Saturdays I do special jobs—extra—but I don't have to work so hard anymore. I have some savings now, and I will have a pension, too. I pay into it, and my employers pay also, and when I cannot work anymore I can draw my pension. Maybe I will go back to Mexico then. I miss it still, and, in many ways, it is very hard to be old in this country. What about you? What kind of work are you doing?"

"I work in a dry cleaner, pressing clothes, oh!"

"Don't worry. I am not going to turn you in to the *migra*. I would not do that, especially not to a compatriot and a woman. But there are people who do those sorts of things, so you have to be careful. I just remembered, you were telling me last time that you did not know where your husband was, or if he was alive. How can that be? ¡*Caramba*! Here comes the bus again. Come on and sit by me, and you can tell me about your situation. Tell me about it quickly, before I have to get off. Perhaps I can help you, even if only with advice."

"Well, Juan—that's my husband—first came across right after our first child was born. Carmelita, you know. Where I come from many of the men go into the mines, but the mines close frequently and, besides, the work is so dangerous. When a man works in the mines, the woman is always afraid that something will happen to him, so I was glad that Juan did not work in the mines, like one of my brothers does. But it is very hard to make a living anywhere else. Juan sometimes worked in construction, like my brother, Mario, and like my father. He was a stonemason—my father, that is—a master mason, but he dislocated something in his back and could not work after he turned fifty."

"Yes, but your husband?"

"Mario, my younger brother—he is two years younger than I am, but we are very close—Mario came across first and worked for a while at all kinds of jobs until he was caught and sent back. After a while, he decided to cross again, and Juan decided to come with him. I did not want him to leave us—me and his little daughter, practically newborn—but what choice was there? We were always hungry. Juan and Mario were both gone for about a year. Then they returned with some money and stayed for a while. They had been sending money all along, not much, but enough to put food on the table. And that's the way it was, over and over. Mario and Juan would be gone for almost a year; then they would come back with a little money and stay until it would run out, and then they would leave again. And after Juan would leave, I would find out that I was expecting a baby. That happened three times; I had a miscarriage once. And I would have my babies while he was gone."

"That must have been very hard for you."

"It was, but my mother helped me . . . They always stayed together—Juan and Mario—and they usually went to California. That's where they would cross. That was where there were plenty of jobs, they said. I was not so worried about Juan then because my brother looked after him, and I thought that Mario would also tell me if Juan had gotten himself another woman. But, suddenly, almost two years ago, according to Mario, Juan decided to leave California, where they had been working in construction, and go to

Texas with some friend. It was a man that he had met on the job, who told him that there were better opportunities in Texas, and he left with this man. Mario did not want to worry me, so at first he did not tell me about it, but when I did not hear from Juan in months, and I had no money, I wrote to Mario and asked him what was happening. Then Mario told me. We did not know how to go about searching for Juan. All we knew was that Juan and his friend had talked about going somewhere near Houston. We did not want to alert the authorities and have him picked up and sent back. He would have been very angry, and, besides, if he had a job, we did not want him to lose it."

"My stop is coming up. This is getting to be like a soap opera. You will have to tell me the conclusion on Thursday. Goodbye, I hope that you have a good day."

"Good morning. I am glad that you got here early. Look, I brought some *empanadas*. Which would you prefer? These are filled with apple and these others with pumpkin. They are from a bakery near my house. They are good, almost like home-made."

"Thank you. I will take apple. I like apples very much. That is one of the best things in this country: the apples. So big and juicy. In Mexico, all you can find are the little ones that are not very sweet."

"Now, tell me the rest of your story."

"Where was I?"

"About your husband. That he had left California and said that he was coming to Texas. And that you had not heard from him in months. What happened to him?"

"Well, that's it. I don't know. Not for sure. Mario tried to get news from him or about him through people who were coming to Texas or had relatives here, but he got nothing. Then, one day, Mario said, he got a letter from the man who had been Juan's friend, the one who brought him to Texas. His name is Armando Saldívar. In the letter he told my brother that he thought he should know, in case he had not been notified, that Juan was dead. He had been killed in a fight outside a bar. Juan and some men had been drinking, and a fight had started, and someone had stabbed Juan . . . once, through the heart. This Armando had not seen it happen, but someone who had been there had told him about it."

"Jesus, Mary and Joseph! What a tragedy! What did you do then?"

"I did not know all this at first, of course. Mario wrote a letter, telling me about it. Mario always wrote regularly to my mother every two weeks, but this time he wrote to me, so right away when I saw the letter, I knew that something bad had happened. As soon as I read it, everything went black before my eyes, and I sat down to keep from fainting and falling down. I was alone with my little girls. When my vision cleared up and I could say something, I sent Carmelita to call my neighbor. I told my neighbor what had happened, and she sent for my mother. You know, for days I could not even cry. I just had this knot inside my chest with a great, big pain over my heart. I thought about him—about Juan—lying there on the pavement, bleeding, dying. Dying alone, like a dog out in the street, with no one to help him or to hold his hand or say a prayer for him. In a strange place."

"And then what did you do?"

"What could I do? I telephoned Mario in California, long distance, as expensive as that is. He was living in a house with other men who were working over there too, but at first I could not locate him. When I finally talked to him, I asked him for every detail. When had it happened? Where had they buried Juan? Had the authorities caught the murderer? He did not know the answers. All he knew was what the man had said in his letter, but he would try to find out the answers to my questions. Mario said that he would be coming home for Christmas, and maybe he would have some answers by then."

"What terrible anguish you must have gone through!"

"At night I would lie in bed, sobbing into my pillow so I would not wake up my little girls and scare them. I remember how the year before we had been so happy, expecting Juan and Mario to be home for Christmas, and now, this year, Juan would not be with us. He was lying buried somewhere in a foreign country, with no one there to even put flowers on his grave. And then I could think of him as he had been when he was with me, when I had first met him, when I had married him. And I would long for him. I would see him again—tall and muscular, a handsome man. Serious, you know, not given to laughing and joking, like my brother, Mario. Sometimes even bad-tempered, but quiet mainly, even when he had been drinking. But when he smiled, he would look so happy, almost like a child. I remembered his hands—calloused from work—when he would touch me and how he smelled of soap after he took a bath."

"You loved him very much."

"I think so. He had his faults, like all men, But I was very happy when I married him. Because we had a proper wedding ceremony, in the church and everything. I insisted on that. Everybody was surprised when he started paying attention to me, because I was not particularly pretty or smart. I was quite tall when I was growing up, and very skinny and terribly shy, but then, when I turned fifteen, I started filling out, you know. I was still slender, but I developed big breasts and nice hips. Still, my family thought of me as the Cinderella, because all I had ever done since I had had to leave school after the fifth grade was to stay home and look after the house and my brothers and sisters. I also used to have a slight cast in my left eye. You can't tell now, unless you are looking very closely, but I did then."

"I can't tell at all, not even looking for it. But why did you have to stay at home when you were a child?"

"There were eight of us, and I was the fifth one. There were two brothers and two sisters ahead of me, but they had already started working, and some were about to get married when my father hurt his back. My mother then had to find work outside the house to help support the family, and she

pulled me out of school when I was about eleven so I could
look after Mario, who was two years younger than me, and
my two little sisters, Leticia and Graciela, and cook and keep
house for all of them. My mother thought that it would not
make any difference if I did not go to school anymore, because
I was not very bright and did not make good grades, anyway.
So there I was, staying at home when Mario started working,
and one day he brought home a friend from the job. It was
Juan."

"Was it love at first sight?"

"Not for him. At first he hardly noticed me, and when he
did, I think he mainly wanted me to go to bed with him, but I
held out. My sisters had had church weddings, and I was not
going to be left out. Later on, my little sister, Leticia, made a
mistake with a man, and she now has two children, and he
never married her. She has to take care of those children
alone. Well, I guess I am alone now, too; but I think it is different . . . being a widow, I mean."

"And what happened when your brother came home?"

"He did not have much more information than before, but
he had heard from this woman who was a cousin of that
Armando Saldívar from Texas. She told Mario that Armando
had sent her something to give to him. It was a cutting from
an old newspaper in Texas, just a short thing, a few lines that
said, according to her, since it was in English, that a man had
been killed, stabbed outside a place called the Acapulco Bar.
It said that the man's name was Juan Emilio Rodríguez and
that he was twenty-six years old and that they were waiting
for someone to claim his body for burial. No arrests had been
made yet. Well, how could we claim him if we did not know?
But the important thing was this, as I told Mario: It had all
been a mistake, someone else had been killed. The age was
right: Juan would have been almost twenty-six then,
although he had not had his birthday yet. He is a year
younger than me. But his name is not Juan Emilio. His name
is Juan Eulalio. It had to be someone else. For a moment I
was so relieved, but then Mario told me that he had already
thought of that and checked back with Armando—he had

managed to talk to him long distance. Armando had explained to Mario that Juan had been carrying some papers that gave him the right to work in the United States . . ."

"A social security card, probably."

"That's right. Armando said that Juan had bought those papers from a man, and that when he bought the papers he had told Armando that his name was not Emilio, but that the initial was the same so that it did not matter."

"My goodness, what a mystery. And did you find out if it was him for sure?"

"No. That is why I am here, . . . in part, I mean."

"Yes, what made you decide to come all the way here, by yourself?"

"I came across the border with my brother. What was I going to do, now that I had to support my children by myself? I was not so afraid because I was with Mario, but it was still a terrifying journey. We were a bunch of poor pilgrims, wandering in the desert. First we came by bus to the border. It was hot there, even though it was still winter, but someone said it would have been much worse in the summer. Many of the men who come here cross a lot of the distances on foot, especially in Texas. They are always in danger of being bitten by snakes, and sometimes they go without food or water for days, always exposed to the elements, Mario said. We crossed in California, which was not as bad. There were many women crossing, too. Women like myself who have to support families. I hope that I do not have to go through that again, but I guess that if I have to, I will. We had a guide, a coyote. He led us across safely. We paid him, of course, but we were lucky that he was honest. Some of those coyotes take your money, I heard, and then leave you to die in the desert or just abandon you anywhere, but this one did what he promised to do, and we got across safely, but it was still a terrible experience. Hiding in the brush, like we were criminals, squatting down in a ditch so the patrol would not see us, walking through mud and getting all scratched by thorns in the brush, always afraid that they would shine a big light on you and round you up and send you back."

"It was certainly an odyssey, as Father Ordóñez used to say. And then you made your way to Texas. You must tell me how that came to be, but here is the bus, and it looks so full that I don't think we will find two seats together. If we cannot, then I will see you next week, and you can finish telling me your story."

IV

"Ah, there you are. I looked for you on Tuesday, but I didn't see you. Did you miss the bus?"

"No, I did not go to work on Monday or Tuesday. Can you believe it? I am never sick, but this time I came down with a cold—in the middle of the summer too—on Friday night, and it was so bad, I got congestion of the chest and I was in bed till Tuesday. It is all this air conditioning. Some places are like refrigerators."

"Yes, I can tell now from your voice that you are still congested. Are you sufficiently recovered?"

"I think so, thank you. You cut your hair! It looks very good with a shape like that."

"You recommended that I do it. I had always worn it long. Juan liked it that way, but you are right. It is not practical to have my hair long in this heat, especially as hot as it is at work, even with the fans, with all those presses."

"Now, tell me what has been happening to you. You had been telling me about how you came to be in Texas."

"Well, when I first came across I stayed with Mario in California. He helped me find a job there. I worked in the kitchen of a restaurant, chopping vegetables—lettuce, tomatoes, onions—and making guacamole all day long. At night I was so tired from being on my feet all day. And I was so sad, too. I would think of my little girls that I had left behind. Now I thought that I could understand what Juan must have felt when he was away from us. Up till now I had known the loneliness and the uncertainty of being left behind—would he be safe, would he forget us? But now I could also understand *his* loneliness, away from home and family, in a strange country where they say that you have no right to be. I remembered how it was when our little boy died. He had caught the measles, and it turned into pneumonia, and we did not have money at the time to get him to the doctor quickly. You can imagine my grief at losing him, but then I had to call Juan in California and tell him. He had been without a job for some weeks, and that was why he had not sent us any money. When he came home the next time, I would see him sit for hours in the house, doing nothing except holding my little boy's stuffed toys in his lap. Juan was never the same after that. All these thoughts would go through my mind at night, and I would fear that something would happen to my little girls while I was gone. I saved all the money I could every month and sent it to my mother, who was keeping my little girls. I got most of my meals at the restaurant and only spent money on rent and on a few clothes. I was living next door to Mario, in an old house where a woman rented out rooms to other women like me. I saw him almost every day, which was a comfort."

"Why did you decide to leave California?"

"That was one thing that I did not tell Mario at first: that I had come with him not only to earn money for my children, but also so that I could try to find out more about Juan. I wanted to meet that woman who was a cousin of Juan's friend, Armando. One day I finally asked Mario to take me to see her. He did, although at first he had a hard time finding her. Her name was Lupe, and she was very nice. She said that she would communicate with her cousin and ask him anything that I wanted. So I asked her to ask him, the next time she wrote to him, or talked to him to give her a description of the man who had been killed. What I really wanted to do was to meet this man, Armando, some day, and show him a photograph of Juan—actually just a snapshot of Juan and Mario—and see if he could recognize him. I did not want to send him the photograph through the mail because it could get lost, but I would show it to him in person."

Beatriz de la Garza

"And did he describe your husband accurately?"

"The description he sent back to Lupe sounded like Juan, but I still was not convinced. When I had left my home to cross the border, I had asked the Virgin of San Juan de los Lagos to protect me and to help me find my husband, and I made a vow that, if I found him, I would make a pilgrimage to her shrine in San Juan. Now I prayed to the Virgin that I could find a way to see this man, Armando Saldívar, and show him the photograph. And at night I would dream that he would see the photo and tell me that it was not the same man as the one that had been killed, and that he knew where my Juan was. The Virgin must have answered my prayers because some time later Lupe told me that she was leaving for Texas, where her cousin, Armando, still lived. On an impulse, I asked her if I could come with her, and she said, yes, and that she would help me find a job here because she had many friends. I took some of the money that I had been saving and bought a bus ticket for Texas and told Mario that I was leaving with Lupe. He was not pleased about it, but he finally understood that I had to try to find out what had happened. At least I could learn where my husband was buried and take some flowers to his grave, if I found out that he was not alive."

"And, have you found out?"

"We got here a month ago, and Armando was then working on a job out of town. We rented—Lupe and I—a room from his mother. Now Lupe got reconciled with her husband and moved out to live with him, but I am still in Doña María's house waiting for Armando to return. He is supposed to be back this weekend, and Doña María has assured me that he will stay with her and that I will meet him then. I can show him the photograph and finally learn the truth."

"The other day I said that this was like a soap opera, and it is. Every time that I see you, you get to tell me only part of the story, and then you leave me waiting for the next episode."

"You know, now that I am so close to finding out the truth, I don't know if I want to. For almost two years I have

The CANDY VENDOR'S BOY

lived with this uncertainty, and now I am afraid of what I will find out. Up till now I have had hope. After this weekend I might not even have that anymore."

"I am not a very religious woman. I go to Mass on Sundays and to confession and communion once a month, but I am not in and out of church every day, like some do. Still, I will pray for you this Sunday. I will pray that, whatever is the result of your interview with this man, you will find peace of mind and that God will give you the strength to accept whatever you find out."

"Thank you. You have been very good—."

"Never mind. Here comes the bus, and it is crowded again. I hope that we will not have to stand up the whole trip. Come on, you will see, everything will go all right."

V

"Hurry up, woman, you are almost late. What kept you this morning? I have been waving at you since your turned the corner, a block away. Didn't you see me?"

"No . . . the sun was in my eyes."

"Oh . . . Look, I brought some mangoes. They are from the big supermarket that just opened last week. Take one or two."

"No, thank you."

"I insist. Eat them for lunch—for dessert, I mean. And now tell me about this weekend. What happened? Was it bad news?"

"Well . . . I suppose you could say that it was bad news. Juan is dead. I saw his grave . . . I think."

"You think? Never mind, start at the beginning, and I hope that today we will have enough time for the whole story, or else the suspense will kill me. Did you see this man, Armando, on Saturday, or whenever it was?"

"He came in very late on Friday, after I had gone to bed, and he was still sleeping when I left for work on Saturday. I got off work at the cleaners at noon, but then I had promised

Lupe to help her at the motel in the afternoon with the laundry. For extra money, you know. Anyway, it was about five when I got back to Doña María's, and I was hot and sweaty. I was hoping that I would have time to have a bath and change clothes before I saw the man. He was out when I got back so I bathed and changed and sat down to have some fried chicken with Doña María, and he arrived when we had just finished."

"And what happened then?"

"Doña María wanted to make supper for him, but he said that he would eat later, when he went out again. Then Doña María introduced me to him and told him that I had something that I wanted to ask him, and she left us alone then. I told him that I was the wife of a friend of his, but did not tell him the name of the friend. I wanted to make sure that he really knew Juan, that he had not made up things . . . and I showed him the photograph. I asked him if he recognized those two men. He looked at the photo for some time and then called to his mother to bring him a beer from the refrigerator. I thought that I would die while I waited as he held the photograph, turning it one way and another to look at it in different light. I told you that it was just a snapshot, quite small, of Juan and Mario in a restaurant in Los Angeles. Mario had sent it to me soon after they had left home together. Finally, Armando said, 'I don't remember the name of one of these men, but the one that looks to be the younger one, I'm pretty sure that I met him before, in California, I think, but I just don't remember his name. The other one looks very much like a man I used to know, Juan Rodríguez. He was a friend. I am not absolutely sure, because when I knew Juan, he did not have a moustache.'"

"Did you know that he had shaved off the moustache?"

"No."

"So, then, what?"

"So then I showed him the newspaper story, and he said that now he remembered the name of the other man in the picture. He was Juan's brother-in-law, Mario, and then he snapped his fingers and said that he had just realized who I was, that I must be Juan's widow. He then offered his condolences to me for my husband's death."

"Do you think that he really had not realized till then who you were?"

"I don't know. I have wondered about it."

"What else did he say? And what did *you* say?"

"I told him that I wanted to know about the circumstances of my husband's death. If it was true that he was dead, why had we not been notified by the authorities? Why hadn't *he* told us about it right away?"

"And what did he reply?"

"He told me that it had happened one Saturday night. He and Juan had been out with a group of men, and they had been to several bars. I got the idea that maybe there were some women with them, but he would not say. He only said that he didn't remember if some of the men's girlfriends had been along. He said that Juan had been drinking heavily. Around midnight, Armando told Juan that he was going home because he was tired and asked Juan if he wanted to leave with him, but Juan got angry and told him to leave him alone. So Armando went home, and he did not see Juan again. Armando was staying with his mother, and Juan was somewhere else. A couple of days later, he heard that Juan had been stabbed in a fight that had broken out in the parking lot of the bar where they had been drinking when Armando left them. It had happened about two in the morning."

"But why didn't he notify your brother then?"

"He said that he had thought that Juan would have had identification and information about his family's address with him and that the authorities would have contacted us. He also said that he had left town that week and had been gone for some time. I asked him if he knew what the cause of the fight had been . . . if it had been over a woman, or over money, if he had been robbed, and had his murderer been caught? Armando said that he did not know the cause of the fight. He had not known the men in the group very well; he had just met them through Juan that very night. He also said that the man who had fought with Juan had escaped and was a fugitive. Someone had also told him that it had been Juan who had pulled a knife first."

"Did you believe him?"

"I don't know what to believe. I have no way of finding out. Juan had always been a quiet man, but he could get very angry if someone provoked him . . . If it was not Juan who died that night, then where is he?"

"You are right. Unless he lost his memory or disappeared and changed his name. But what a lot of stupidities I am saying. This is not a novel. What else did you find out?"

"I asked him if he knew where Juan was buried. He thought about that for some time before he said that he did not, but that he could try to find out, that perhaps he could tell me something the following day. Then he went out. You can imagine what kind of night I spent. I hardly slept. All sorts of thoughts kept going through my head. You know what this man, Armando, is like?"

"Tell me about him."

"Well, he is not very tall, and he is thin. He is strong, you can tell, for his size, but not big at all. And when I saw him he was very clean—his clothes, especially his shirt—it was white and freshly starched and ironed. He wore a large, gold medal on a chain and had a gold wrist watch. He smelled of perfumed soap. And his hands, they looked smooth, his nails very clean and trimmed. Do you know what I am trying to say?"

"I think so."

"I don't think that he worked on construction with Juan. But I needed to know where Juan was buried. If he could tell me that, if I could visit his grave, well, then that was all that mattered."

"And did he tell you?"

"Sunday morning, while I was washing up the breakfast dishes, he came in the kitchen and told me that he had found where Juan was buried, and that if I wanted to, he would take me there. Right away. So I dried my hands and went with him."

"You went off with this sinister man! Got in an automobile and went off with him without knowing where you were going?"

"I stopped on the way out and told his mother that he was taking me to the cemetery where my husband was buried. I trust Doña María; she is a good woman. She was just going to Mass then, and she said that she would pray for both Juan and for me."

"And where did you go?"

"I don't know this city very well, so I cannot tell you the direction in which we went, but it was quite far out, on the outskirts of town. There was this big cemetery with rows and rows of narrow tombstones—just plain. No crosses, no statues of saints, no flowers to show that anybody remembered those dead. I felt very bad that I had not brought even a single flower with me. We left the car and started walking among those rows of tombstones. It was so desolate there. I was afraid that the man I was with was going to kill me and leave me there, perhaps put me in one of those graves. I tell you, the place was so strange that it put all sorts of thoughts in my head. I finally asked him what kind of cemetery this was, and he said that it was where the authorities buried those people that nobody claimed. I felt as if a knife had gone through my heart. My poor Juan, buried like that, as if he had been a beggar, without family or friends. Perhaps I could take him back home, but I knew that was out of the question. I would never have the money to pay for that."

"Did you ever find his grave?"

"Yes, but before we did we had to read name after name on those narrow little markers. Just a little piece of metal, you know, with a name, and sometimes a date of birth—not always—and the date of death. And there it finally was: 'Juan E. Rodríguez' and the date of birth, which was not right, because he had somebody else's papers, you know. And the date of death. And that was all."

"And now that you have visited the tomb of Juan E. Rodríguez—was it Juan Emilio or Juan Eulalio?"

"I think that I must accept that I have found Juan, don't you agree?"

"I don't see what else you can do. And now, what will you do?"

"I am going home. I have not seen my daughters in over a year. Last night, I dreamed that I was back with them, but that they did not recognize me. I had been gone so long. You know, those long absences change people. It is the time that passes and what happens when people are gone. I told you that Juan was never the same after our little boy died. I wonder if Juanito's death would have affected him in the same way if he had been there when it happened. Mario told me that he had never understood why Juan had left California, why he took up with this Armando and came to Texas. Juan had a job pretty steadily when he was in California. He did not have a job much of the time when he was in Texas, according to Armando. Armando thought that Juan had just gotten tired of the same routine and decided to see something different, but that was not like Juan at all. It could have all been due to a woman, I suppose. Men often take up with other women when they are away from their wives, but Armando did not say anything about that. Or it could have been something more terrible: some crime or something like that, drugs, maybe. God only knows. I don't think that I can find out any more."

"No, I don't think that you can."

"I am going back home, and I am going to have a Mass said for his soul, that it may have rest. After that I think that I should go to San Juan de los Lagos, to the shrine, to fulfill my vow to the Virgin. I vowed that I would make a pilgrimage to her shrine, don't you remember?"

"My dear . . . don't you think that you have been on a pilgrimage all this time? Never perching on a green branch, like the turtledove . . . ?"

"But I have found him . . . and that was what I had prayed to the Virgin to grant me. I must keep my promise."

"And when you have seen your daughters and made your pilgrimage, what will you do then? Will you come back?"

"I don't know . . . I probably will. I will still need to find work to support myself and my children, and if I cannot find it there . . . Perhaps some day I will bring my daughters back with me. Perhaps we will all be able to have a home together here."

Pilgrimage

"Will you write to me when you are gone? I will give you my address. And when you decide to come back, will you let me know? I will help you if I can . . ."

"Yes, I know. And I will write to you. I will not feel so sad when I leave my daughters if I know that . . . that I have a friend waiting here."

"Here is the bus now. It is running late this morning."

Pillars of
Gold and Silver

*T*he thought comes to Stella that afternoon that perhaps she dislikes the child. "Nonsense," she tells herself, "I am a teacher. I like children. I am a teacher because I like children." On their own, though, her steps slow down as she approaches the classroom where he waits for her. She looks at him through the window, sitting in a miniature chair. He is too big for the kindergarten furniture and yet too small for his age. No child should look like that, she thinks, noticing the resigned angle of the shoulders, the hopelessness of the hands in his lap.

They go through the hour-long drill, as they have done for the last month, almost every afternoon of the school week. "This is a pencil," holding up a pencil. "This is a pen. Pencil—*lápiz*. Book—*libro*. I open a window," as she walks to the window and tugs with it. "*La ventana*—the window." She uses the flash cards; she acts out verbs. "What is your name? *¿Cómo te llamas?* My name is Paul. *Me llamo Pablo*. I am Paul. *Yo soy Pablo*."

She repeats the phrases, usually first in English, then in her slow, careful Spanish. The child sits silently, an apologetic expression on his face, as if he were sorry to be troubling her this way. He regrets that she has to stay late after school just for him. He is even a little embarrassed for her as she exaggerates the actions that she is illustrating: "I open the door. I sit down. I stand up." Throughout it all he remains in his island of silence. He wants no part of this activity on his behalf.

He had been this way ever since his arrival, some three months ago, his aunt said, when she brought him to school.

He might as well not speak any language. His aunt looked middle aged, although she could not have been more than thirty-five. He was nine, very close to ten, she thought. The parents were dead. A violent death such as seemed endemic South of the Border, from the Rio Grande to Patagonia. Death from revolution or political repression, crime or undifferentiated violence—it all amounted to the same, Stella had thought as she sat through the interview with Pablo's guardian, translating between the aunt and the school principal.

The hour-lesson is over, and she tells him it is time to go. This, being Friday, she also wishes him a good weekend. She speaks to him in English, hoping to trick him into revealing that he has understood her, but he does not move. His body stiffens in the ignominiously small chair, but he remains still, like an animal that has been trapped before and now does not trust his instincts. She repeats the dismissal in Spanish, and this time he gets up and walks out of the room with that odd gait of his that is almost a shuffle.

She leans back in her chair and closes her eyes. Does the child have a speech impediment, after all? Does he have a learning disability, the term now favored over retardation? She knows that, in the past, children who did not speak English were labeled as retarded due to lack of speech development in a foreign language. But that happened in the dark ages, before schools became enlightened to the needs of the foreign children who had begun appearing at the school doors. How had they done it before, when the waves of Slavs and Italians were arriving at Ellis Island? They had somehow learned English. I did it, after all, she thinks, as she stands up briskly and begins collecting her handbag and her notebook.

She says good night to the custodian and wishes him a good weekend. He is a black man in his sixties, a pleasant, soft-spoken man of unlimited patience with the all-female teaching staff and their problems of jammed locks, windows that stick and even an occasional stalled car. She usually stops to chat with him, but this afternoon she is tired and wants only to go home.

Her white compact car is one of only three still left in the parking lot. The other two belong to the custodian and to the principal. She drives away from the school with its modern brick and glass architecture and into the wide, tree-lined streets with their graceful houses from an earlier time. The school is named after the community: Walnut Hills Elementary School. Walnut Hills. Stella loves the name and loves the place. She has been there five years, and she still enjoys going home after school, past the two-story houses with their ever-fresh coats of paint, bright shutters, deep verandas, precisely clipped hedges and full-canopied trees in their yards.

These are the streets where Dick and Jane once walked with their dog, Spot, where Judy Garland sang about the boy next door and looked for the yellow brick road. Golden haired children play in these yards and go to school at Walnut Hills Elementary. Golden haired children, she thinks, and one little boy with sallow skin and unblinking black eyes and the pinched mouth of a prematurely old child. Why has he come here? Why has she agreed to tutor him after school? He came here against his will, she answers herself. He came here because he could not stay where his parents had died—in southern Mexico or Guatemala or some other Central American country where they always have unrest. Somebody decided that he should come here, to be safe with his relatives, but he left his heart behind, wherever it was that he came from. And for that reason I tutor him . . . because at least I share a language with him. No, she rebuts herself, he has a language of his own that I don't understand.

She turns slowly into the neat, gravel drive that leads up to the brick, two-story house with green shutters. She lives on the second floor. Mr. Kirk, her landlord, is trimming a few stray wisps from the otherwise well-disciplined hedge, while his wife plants a bed of chrysanthemums. She waves at both of them before disappearing into the garage behind the house. She then climbs the wrought-iron spiral staircase in the back and lets herself in through the kitchen door.

The apartment is Stella's inner sanctum. When she comes home in the evening and closes the door behind her, a sense of peace descends on her. Perhaps it is the high ceilings and the long windows that open the rooms to the tree tops outside. Besides the kitchen of gleaming black and white tile, she has a large living and dining room combination, a spacious bedroom and a small study. The walls are white throughout and the hardwood floors shine with polish brightened by a bright blue and green rug that makes an island of color in front of the living room sofa. Every object in the apartment has been carefully selected by her, from the shiny copper teakettle on the stove to the needlepoint pillows on the ivory-hued sofa. On the walls are framed reproductions of Sargent's women with opalescent skins and pink and white children by Renoir.

Today Stella resists the impulse to drop her handbag and notebook on the glass-topped coffee table. She carries them, instead, to their appointed place on the desk in the study. In the bedroom she removes her clothes and deposits them in a wicker hamper and then puts on a heavy cotton caftan. She walks barefooted to the living room, uncertain, for once, as to what to do next. She looks out the front window and sees her landlords gathering their gardening tools. It is no more than five o'clock, but the early autumn sun already falls obliquely across the lawn, and she knows the air has a chill to it.

At least once a month, usually on a Friday evening, she invites the Kirks who live downstairs to have dinner with her. It gives her great satisfaction to prepare for them some deceptively simple meal with the freshest herbs, the best ingredients—perhaps a fragrant bouillabaisse or chicken and dumplings with flaky biscuits and homemade pie for dessert—so that the Kirks go home downstairs delighted, but a little puzzled as to why such a wonderful housekeeper is not married yet. She takes the same pains with her meals when she eats alone, as she does most evenings. Then, it may be a perfect Caesar salad or a broiled steak, if she is very hungry, and a glass of wine—but only one. After that it is music on the stereo, perhaps Mozart, and a book if she does not have lessons to prepare.

This evening Stella has the absurd craving for a cup of hot chocolate. Not cocoa, though, she realizes, but that cinnamon-flavored chocolate of her childhood long ago. She rejects the whim and decides that what she needs is a bath before dinner. She is tired and tense from the week and needs to relax. She fills the tub, sprinkling aromatic bath salts in it, and later, sitting submerged in the tepid water up to her shoulders, closes her eyes and tells her mind to go blank. Pablito's face floats in front of her, instead. She opens her eyes and realizes that she is angry. Why? Is it because he gives her a sense of failure, because she cannot teach him? No, not that. She cannot reach him.

What is he doing here? What is his family doing in Walnut Hills? Are there others like them? These people, like troubles, never come singly, she knows. Out of several hundred children in her school, there are perhaps a handful of black faces, the children of professionals. In the fourth grade there are two little Japanese girls, dainty little dolls whose father is a physicist. The poor immigrants—Latin Americans, mostly, but also a few Asians, stay in the city or the suburbs closer to it, where their jobs are. What is Pablo's family doing here?

She does not mind the challenge or the hard work. Once she had worked successfully with an autistic child that everyone else had given up on. Her supervisors often comment on how she is always ready to go the extra mile, do extra work such as tutoring this child. Pablo is not her student. He belongs in the third grade, but that does not mean anything because he can sit in the third grade forever and never understand what is going on until he learns English.

When the third-grade teacher had seen what Pablo's problem was (or what she thought it was), she had gone to Mrs. Patterson, the principal. Mrs. Patterson had, naturally, asked Stella to help. Stella had minored in Spanish in college, hadn't she? Had spent some time in Mexico, as well? Stella had said that she would be glad to help, but that her

Spanish was a little rusty. Never mind, it will all come back quickly to you, Mrs. Patterson had been confident. And it has.

These people, she thinks, as she towels herself furiously, bring their misery with them, like turtles carrying their shells on their backs.

She steps into her bedroom and stands in front of the mirror, brushing back her hair as her bare feet sink into the deep pile of a sheepskin rug. On the dresser there are two groups of photographs. In the large one her lovely mother sits surrounded by her men. There is Poppy, standing behind her, with a hand on her shoulder, and the smiling twins, fourteen years old at the time, flanking her at each side. A good looking family. The smaller photograph shows Stella in her high school graduation cap and gown and her mother and Poppy at her side.

*

Poppy, she thinks, darling Poppy, who made so many things possible for me, who gave me what I wanted most— his name. He thought it was his love that I wanted, and I did, I did. I loved him dearly, but I coveted his name, and my mother's name, and the name of the twins. They were Mr. and Mrs. Mills, and the twins were Ben and Bill Mills. But to the teachers and the kids at school I was "the little Benavides girl, the little Mexican Benavides girl." Except that they could never pronounce the name and said it with every possible distortion, and the other kids sometimes laughed at me because of that.

She had been profoundly grateful, even if a little ashamed of herself, when she had heard Poppy asking Lili, her mother, if Stella would mind if he adopted her. "I overheard her saying her name was Stella Mills. I thought she meant that she wanted to be my daughter. I don't imagine that she remembers her father. She was very young when he died, wasn't she? I imagine, too, that she would like to have the same name as the rest of us. What do you think, Lili?"

And her mother saying, "Why don't we ask her?" Stella had said yes.

Poppy was ice cream and cake on those Sunday afternoons when despair had crept like a fog into the small apartment where Stella lived with her mother and filled every corner with its suffocating grayness. She did not remember when he first came to see the two of them, only that after a while silence did not hang over them, mother and daughter, while the woman darned her clothes and washed her hair, and the little one pretended to nap on those interminable Sundays. Now there was Poppy arriving at three o'clock with a birthday cake for Stella and cartons of beautiful pink ice cream with strawberry bits in it. She had never had a birthday cake before. There was fruit as well and other things she could no longer remember, the way she still remembered the chocolates wrapped in gold paper. Lili would protest, but he would silence her, saying, "It's nothing. Absolutely nothing. They practically give them away at the PX."

Stella had known that the gifts, even the birthday cake were really for her mother. She, herself, was not a particularly engaging child, with long, skinny legs, heavy pigtails and too serious an expression on her pale face. It was her mother who brought forth tribute—her mother with the face like a magnolia blossom and the hair of midnight black that rose in two wings from her temples.

(Poppy had taken Lili's hands in his and was speaking to her, trying to look into her eyes, but she would not look at him. Stella wanted to tell him that her mother's eyes were like the ocean that he had taken them to see. Some days they were gray and some days green, or even gold, and sometimes they were almost black.)

"He has asked me to marry him. What do you think I should say?" her mother confided in Stella. They both turned to look at the photograph on the dresser of the handsome soldier that looked back at them with a rakish smile.

"He was at Inchon, you say?" she had heard Poppy ask, early on. "A lot of good men were lost there." Stella had wondered if her father was still lost and if anybody was out looking for him. She had concluded that they did not expect to find her father.

At the wedding they had found out that Poppy's name was Ernest, but everybody called him Pop, even his new wife, who was almost twenty years younger than he. He had asked Stella what she should call him, and she had looked with gratitude at the plain-looking man with the sandy hair and eyebrows who thought that she mattered. Inspiration came to her out of nowhere, and she had said, "Poppy." A loving compromise, perhaps. "Poppy" he was to her since then.

The twins had come about a year later, after they moved into a house. Her mother had given up her job. Poppy had taken on a second job because, even with his military pension, it was hard to make ends meet with a young family. Stella loved the twins and delighted in helping her mother with them. She was ten when they were born and was soon old enough to babysit them. They were rowdy and boisterous children, such as she could never have been. They were not weighed down by history.

When Stella graduated from high school, she knew that, if she wanted to go on to college, she would have to pay for it. She took out a student loan and headed east, away from the borders where the extremes meet, where the jagged edges of wounds never heal, toward the great expanses of the heartland that promised anonymity and oblivion. She wanted to be engulfed by the country, to be as American as the name of Stella Mills and a medium complexion would let her be. People there might look at her brown hair and eyes and light olive complexion, but the thought "Mexican" did not cross their minds anymore than "Greek" or "Argentine." She was simply Stella Mills, college student, and later Stella Mills, teacher, all the past washed away by the great river of the Midwest.

Two years ago Poppy had died, and, as she had stood at his graveside, she had cried without restraint, pouring out tears of gratitude and affection for him. Now the twins were almost seventeen. When they finished high school they would probably go into the Navy, like their daddy, according to Lili. Lilia wondered if, when she was alone, she ought to go back home. Stella wanted to argue with her: "How can you call it home, when you have not been there in twenty years?"

☆

Supper tonight is a sandwich and a can of soup—most unlike her. Afterwards, to give herself something to do, she decides to hem up a skirt. She finds the skirt and gets the sewing box out of her closet. It is an old fashioned metal box for chocolates, with a reproduction, in sepia tone, of the Grand Canal of Venice on the lid. As she holds it in her lap the years fall away suddenly, and she is again sorting through the box, amazed by the wealth of buttons inside it: pearl buttons, horn buttons, brass and pewter buttons. Her grandmother would let her play with the buttons as a very special treat. She puts the box away and goes to bed.

Her consciousness hovers on the surface of sleep, like a body only half submerged in the water. The emptiness of the apartment closes in on her. She wishes that she had a cat to keep her company, warm her feet in bed. Tomorrow she will see about getting a cat. She dreams that she has brought home a beautiful white Persian, but that he keeps escaping out the window. She wakes up and remembers that she has left the skirt only halfway hemmed. Tomorrow, she must finish hemming it.

In the first cold light of dawn she finally goes completely under, sinking to the bottom of the well, into the very heart of sleep. There she finds herself sorting buttons. She is sewing buttons on a jacket, a military jacket. She is short one silver button. She empties the button box on the floor, and the metal buttons scatter and glitter in the moonlight. She can hear the children singing outside. She steps forward to join them, but the iron bars at the window press against her cheek and hold her in. She had forgotten that she is in the small recess between the heavy shutters that someone has closed behind her and the iron grillwork that juts out into the street. She holds out her hand through the bars to reach them, but the children do not see her. Under a bright moon they are singing, hands linked in a circle: "*Doña Blanca está encerrada . . .*"

Then she sees the little girl with the heavy pigtails standing inside the circle, and she thinks to herself, "Why, that looks like Blanca Estela." The children are going away now, riding in the back of a truck, its bed filled with woolly cotton bales. They perch on top of the cotton bales, and it is early morning now, and they call out, "Blanca Estela, come out and play," or is it, "Blanca Estela, *ven a jugar?*"

She wakes up. She touches her cheeks where the iron grillwork had pressed against them, and they are wet. She is still crying when the sun comes in through the eastern window and makes a warm patch of yellow on her bed. She gets up, wrapping herself in a quilted robe against the chill of the morning, and makes coffee. While the coffee drips, she finds a legal-size pad and a pen from the study and sets them down on the kitchen table.

"What was it like? What was it really like? I must remember. I must write it all down," she whispers feverishly. "I must write a record, try to remember it all and write it down before it all dies inside me. But . . . what language? It all happened in another language." How often she has heard, and even used, the term "mastering a language," as if language were an animal that you domesticated. You went about your daily tasks, harnessing a language, as if it were a placid draft horse that served you well in your mundane chores, although he never even lifted you very far above the ground. But the other one—the high-spirited animal that carried you with the wind—you only mastered him, if at all, if you were a superb rider.

"Never mind. Never mind the language. It will come as it will," and she sits down, coffee cup in the left hand and pen in the right, to write.

★

It was the summer of nineteen fifty something. Fifty-two or fifty-three, somewhere around the time when people began wearing buttons that said "I Like Ike," that the men came to the little house and brought a little box with medals and ribbons in it. They gave the box to the young woman, but it did not make her happy. She looked at the medals, and she began to cry. Other people came too, and embraced the beautiful young woman, and sometimes they all cried. Sometimes they would also remember the little girl and give her hugs too. The little girl would often hide in the kitchen when the people came. She hated to see them cry, and she was frightened when she heard the grown-ups weeping.

One day the young woman and the little girl packed their suitcases and got on a bus. They left behind them the emerald lawns and the flower boxes, the sea that roared just out of hearing and the blue mountains in the distance and rode into the heat and the grays and browns of the desert. They rode for several days as sweat trickled down their backs and their thin dresses clung to their seats. They would stop sometimes and get out to stretch their legs under the blazing sun or go eat sandwiches in dim little stores that smelled of coffee and spices. They rode over mountains and past landscapes pocked with craters and dunes and over hills and across little streams. The little girl slept a great deal of the time.

Then they were getting out again, and this time their suitcases were unloaded. It was very hot. The little girl had never felt heat like that. It was like standing in front of the oven when you opened it to take out the cookies. Her mother was talking to a fat woman inside the little store that also had gasoline pumps outside. There was a bench just outside the door, and the little girl sat down to wait for her mother to come out. She could hear her talking inside. They were talking in Spanish. She knew it was Spanish because that was what her mother spoke to her at home. Nobody else around them did. The little girl understood what her mother said to her, but she wanted to talk like June and Linda, who were her best friends from next door. They spoke English and so did their mother. *Her* own mother would also speak English when they went shopping or when she talked to the neighbors. She spoke it funny, though, and said some things wrong, but she was such a pretty and sweet young woman that nobody minded much, and they all thought it was cute the way she talked.

The man by the gasoline pumps was calling to the people inside the store that the car was coming, and her mother and the fat woman came out, and her mother asked her if she needed to go to the bathroom and hurried her into the little cubicle inside. Her mother knew the driver, and they talked as they loaded the suitcases in the trunk. Her mother rode in the front seat with him, and the little girl had the back seat to herself. The leather seat cover was cracked, and the springs sagged as they drove away. After a while they turned off the paved road and took a dirt track.

The little girl looked back, but all she could see was the cloud of dust that they trailed behind. Suddenly there was a hanging bridge ahead of them. She became terrified when she saw it swaying in the wind and realized that they were going to cross it. Her mother did not seem worried, though, and continued talking to the driver. The girl looked down and saw a sullen, brown river, slithering over large, flat rocks between the sandy banks. Then they were across the river, and two men in khaki uniforms stopped the car and talked to the driver and to her mother. She saw her mother laugh for the first time in a long time. The men waved them on.

She saw something white shimmering in the distance. The driver, who was a big, gray-haired man with a brown face, turned to speak to the little girl in the back seat and, pointing ahead with one hand, said, "That's Revilla just ahead." She nodded politely. It did not mean anything to her.

They drove down a long, dusty street lined with houses made of stone, whose walls rose like cliffs directly from the street. Some of the houses were whitewashed, and the glare from the sun which they reflected dazzled her eyes. Others had exposed sandstone blocks where the stucco had peeled off and had a mottled look, like an animal shedding its fur. They had massive wooden doors that sometimes stood half-open and door-length windows protected by iron bars. Nothing stirred in the noonday sun—only a few dogs that huddled close to the walls, looking vainly for shade. She could hear no sound save a chorus of cicadas and the cooing of turtledoves in the distance.

They stopped before one of the mottled houses, and the driver honked his horn. A plump, gray-haired woman wearing a black-and-white print dress came out wiping her hands on a white apron. The little girl remembered that her mother had been wearing nothing but black for some time now. The two women embraced for a long time, and then both began to cry. The little girl leaned back against a corner in the back seat. She did not want to see crying again. Suddenly, the older woman was opening the back door of the car and lifting her out in her arms, kissing her and clasping her against her. The little girl looked at her mother, the question in her eyes.

"It's your grandmother, *tontita*. You silly little thing!"

"What did you expect, Lilia? I haven't seen the child since she was in diapers. I would have known her, anyway. She gets her eyes from Roberto. She takes more after her father's family."

They were standing in a covered entryway that opened into a dusty courtyard—a *patio*, as she came to learn that it was called. Flower pots lined the whitewashed walls of the entrance, and the floor was made of rough paving stones. In the middle of the courtyard stood a stone structure which her grandmother soon identified to her as the cistern from which they took all their water and into which—under no circumstances—was she to lean forward and try to peer into. A metal bucket with an attached rope rested upside down next to the cistern.

It was dinner time, and they had a delicious broth made with beef and cabbage and corn and squash and onions and tomatoes, and they had hot corn tortillas which they shredded and dropped into the soup. It was the first hot meal they had in days, and it made the little girl sleepy. The grand-mother set up a narrow canvas cot in front of an open window and told her to go to sleep. She fell asleep to the murmur of the two women's voices in the next room.

They now lived in this new place where everything was so old. The strangeness of their new life did not overwhelm her as it could have though. She took her cue from her mother. Her mother accepted that lights did not come on at night anymore by flicking a switch, and so did she. Instead, they lighted a kerosene lamp when the sun went down, and if the lamplight threw gigantic shadows against the wall and never reached the far corners of the rooms where the portraits of ancestors brooded in the gloom, this did not frighten her, because her mother was not afraid. Going to the out-house did scare her, but her mother would go with her and stand by until she conquered her revulsion.

Other things were even fun, such as taking a bath in a galvanized tin tub in the kitchen while her mother poured bucketfuls of cold water over her, or sleeping outdoors at night. If it was hot, they would set up canvas cots in the courtyard, secure behind the high walls that surrounded them and the massive doors with their iron bolts. Lying in her cot, the little girl would look up at the sky and ask her mother about the stars above. In the morning, the sun would wake them up as it came over the walls that enclosed the courtyard and dry out the sheets that had become damp with dew during the night.

In the mornings, the two women cleaned house and then cooked the main meal, which was at noon. In the afternoons they sat in the cane-backed rocking chairs and sewed or knit while they talked of relatives that the little girl had never met. While they talked she would look at sepia-tinted pho-tographs pasted in albums or gaze at her parents' wedding portrait. Her mother looked very much the same as in the picture, just a little thinner now, and was very pretty in her white wedding dress. She gazed intently into her father's eyes, seeking to find in them her own that her grandmother had said she had.

She had no recollection of him, just a shadowy memory, more like a dream, of his strong arms holding her high up in the air and then setting her down on his shoulders while he pretended to gallop like a horse. She heard the two women recount the story of her parents' courtship. She heard how Roberto would come across that swaying bridge every Sunday, rain or shine, cold or hot, to promenade with Lilia around the plaza while her brothers stood by the bandstand in the middle of the square and maintained their vigilant watch in place of their dead father. She was their only sister, and they were going to make sure that no one trifled with her.

The brothers, themselves, had since married and left to make a living in the city. They now urged their mother to come and join them where she could be close to them and enjoy the conveniences of modern city life, but she would never leave her house. She knew where she wanted to die, where she wanted to be buried, next to her husband, close to friends and neighbors. She did not want to lie, after death, among strangers, when all her life she had lived among friends.

The older woman would then urge her daughter to come back, if not to her, at least to live close by, among her dead husband's family, across the river. But the young woman would become agitated and say that there was no future down there, on either side of the river, in either country, and, besides, she had never gotten along with Roberto's mother and sisters.

The little girl was a habitually quiet child, but she was even more so now. She did not want to offend her grandmother by speaking to her in a language that she did not understand, but neither did she feel up to addressing her in Spanish. She communicated indirectly, therefore. She would whisper what she wanted, in English, to her mother, who would then translate. Finally, the older woman exploded in irritation: "Lilia, if you don't do something, this child is going to end up mute! I don't know how much English she knows, but I know that you do not know much of it yourself;

and she does not know Spanish. We have to teach her. She has grown up like a plant without roots, like those plants that hang in the air and attach themselves to whatever they find. Give her roots! Teach her what she is and who she is."

After that, her mother encouraged her to say things directly to her grandmother, and she did because she did not want to make her angry. Her vocabulary was getting better from listening to the two women talk every day, and her grandmother seemed pleased. What she would not do was go out to play with the children from the neighborhood. Every evening, after supper and after the sun had gone down, the children would come out to play in the street. They would hold their games in front of any of several houses within a two-block range, and sometimes they played directly in front of her grandmother's house. The little girl would watch them from the embrasure of the window, refusing her grandmother's encouragement to go out and join them. The games involved songs, chants and riddles, linguistic feats that she was not willing to attempt for fear of their ridicule. One evening a little boy, who was the youngest in the large family that lived next door, came to the window and asked her to join them, but she merely shook her head and withdrew hastily from the window. She enjoyed watching them, though, and gradually came to recognize several of the tunes of their games and even learned some of the words.

One day came a shattering blow. Her mother began putting her clothes in her suitcase, and the little girl, thinking their visit was at an end, began to do the same. Her mother stopped what she was doing and, taking her aside, explained that she was going away by herself. Just for a little while, she hastened to add, as she saw the look of horror on her daughter's face. "Estela," she always called her just "Estela," and not "Blanca Estela," as her grandmother did. "Estelita," her mother said, "I am going away for a little while. I have to look for a job to support us. You will stay with your grandmother until I find a job. It will be just for the summer, just for a little while. She will take good care of you, and you will be company for her. She is lonely. And then I will come back for you, and you will start school in English. It will be like we had planned to do—before your father went away." Then she began to weep, but she dried her tears quickly. "Do you remember your father?" How could she tell her about the memory of being held by those strong arms, of the hard muscles under the starched fabric of his shirt when he would hold her up in the air, about the thrill of those gallops on his shoulders? She had probably dreamed it. "You were such a baby when he left," her mother continued. "He went to war, you know, and they killed him there. He was very brave. That was why they brought me those medals, but I don't want the medals. I want him." And then she ran out of the room, and when she came back she finished packing.

Early the next morning the car, which must have been one of only four or five in town, stopped in front of the house. The little girl stood rigidly in front of the massive doors of the *zaguán* as her mother climbed in the front seat with the driver. Only after the car had driven off and her mother had stopped waving back at them did she give in to the overwhelming need to run after it, but her grandmother stopped her just as she was breaking away and held her tightly against her. She tried to push away this hateful old woman that smelled of sun-dried clothes and soap. Stella finally escaped her and hid in the only hiding place afforded by the open, rambling house. She went in the outhouse and latched herself in and only came out when it got too hot inside.

Then it was as if she had finally reached the mute stage that her grandmother had predicted. She would not speak. Her grandmother did not force her to talk either, but spoke to her as though she expected no response. She would ask her to fetch water from the cistern and give her careful instructions so she would not fall in. She would give her a small sack of beans to clean before cooking them. She would ask her to find a particular button in the box with the boating illustration on the lid. She would have her thread a needle for her. In turn, she seemed to guess the little girl's wants and needs. She knew that the little girl disliked the taste of boiled milk, so she would disguise it in frothy, cinnamon-flavored chocolate that she whipped with a wooden whisk. She would brush her hair at night until it soothed her and made her sleepy. In the long afternoons she would read stories and fairy tales to her from a stack of books that always sat on a table in the parlor.

But the grief of abandonment stayed with her. One night she woke up sobbing out of a dream that she could not remember. She only remembered how sad it was. Her grandmother took her in her arms and sat her in her lap and rocked her in the cane-backed chair while she sang to her the lullaby of Saint Anne—the lullaby that Saint Anne had sung to her grandchild, the baby Jesus.

A letter came from her mother on the following day, and the grandmother read it for both of them because the little girl did not yet know how to read. She was not six yet.

That evening Stella left the shelter of the window and stood out on the sidewalk while the children played. The little boy, whose name was Fernando, came to ask her again to join them and even taught her the words to the game they were playing. Under a full moon she sang with them and joined hands with them as they chanted rhymes of games whose counterparts she later learned in another school and another language. They were all barefooted, and she still remembers to this day the feeling of the cool, gritty sand as it burrowed into the crevices between her toes. When it was time to go to bed, her grandmother washed her feet and kissed her good night.

From then on she joined them in their games every night until the mothers came to the doorstep, if they were inside, or took in their chairs, if they were sitting in the *zaguanes* or on the sidewalk, and called them in to go to bed. And later, in the morning, she would hear the rumble of the big truck that came to pick up the children to go to the fields to pick cotton. They earned spending money this way, and she had wanted to join them there, also. Fernando had even offered to teach her how to hold the burlap sack and fill it with cotton bolls, but her grandmother had refused her permission to go with them. "You are not used to being out in this hot weather in the middle of the day. You might get sunstroke." And so they left without her, but in the evenings she would be waiting for them.

One game that they played was about Doña Blanca. The children formed two concentric circles while they held hands, and a child stood in the center of both. She was Doña Blanca, the Lady Blanche. She was a princess shut up in a tower. The children in the outer circle marched in one direction while they sang about the Lady Blanche, who was surrounded by pillars of gold and silver. They would break down a pillar to see the Lady Blanche, they sang, as they tried to break in past the inner circle. Sometimes the arms of the guardians of the inner circle held fast, but sometimes a weak link would be found, and the rescuers would stream in to rescue the Lady Blanche. Doña Blanca was the favored child, the Queen of the May. It was never the little girl, but she did not hold it against them. It would have embarrassed her to be thus singled out.

One day, again at noon, the car brought her mother back. The little girl was ecstatic. She had so much to tell her. She chattered—in Spanish—to her mother about the games and the other children and about how they went picking cotton and earned money doing so, and how the little boy next door, her best friend, was going to start school in September, and she wanted to go to school, too. Her mother was pleased with her, but she also seemed pleased about something else. Her face was not as pale as before, and her eyes were brighter. She was wearing now a black skirt with a white blouse, instead of the black dresses that she had worn before. Late that night, the little girl could hear the two women talking, sitting in the dark before an open window, while she lay in her cot in the courtyard.

The next morning her mother told her that she had come to take her back with her. She had found a job. It was factory work and did not pay much, but, put together with her widow's pension, they could manage. She, her darling Estelita, would start school in September—in English—and she would make new friends. "But I was going to go to school with Fernando," was her only response. Her mother explained again. She would go to school in English, on the other side. "Will June and Linda be there, too?" she wanted to know. No, they were going to live in another town. There would be new friends. A vague apprehension settled over her, coupled with a feeling of importance. She told the other children that night that she would soon be leaving to go to school "across the river, far away—in English."

The evening before they left, she was chosen to be Doña Blanca. As she stood in the center of the two circles, she felt happy. The children on the outer circle wanted to reach her and be her rescuers; the ones on the inside wanted to keep her for themselves. They sang: *Doña Blanca está encerrada / en pilares de oro y plata. / Romperemos un pilar / para ver a Doña Blanca.* It did not matter who won. What mattered was that they wanted her.

The next day she kissed her grandmother goodbye and promised to write to her very, very soon, as soon as she learned how to. She promised to come back next summer. She promised Fernando that she would go picking cotton with him next year. And as they drove away, she clasped in her lap the precious button box with the most precious buttons in it—her grandmother's farewell gift.

On the return journey, men in green uniforms stopped them on the far side of the bridge. These men did not smile or make conversation with her mother. They merely looked at the papers that she showed them and asked her many questions, first in broken Spanish and then in English, until the pretty young woman became irritated and had to bite her lip to control her temper. Finally, they waved them on without a smile.

Then there was a new town and a new home—a small apartment where there was not much light and little room to move in. There was school, too, for the first time. It was a school where they only spoke one language, the language that she had almost forgotten, and which did not have words for many things. There were friends, eventually, to play with on the playground, but none to play with by the moonlight. She was never again the Lady Blanche.

Then came Poppy and a new family. Her grandmother died soon after the twins were born, and none of them went to the funeral.

And I never went back. She died, and she is buried now among her friends and next to her husband. Who tends those graves now? Perhaps the uncles who are now strangers forever, perhaps the cousins that I never met. Perhaps now Lilia hears the call of voices from across the years and across the miles and knows that things always return to their beginnings. But I never went back. Not the following summer to pick cotton with Fernando. Not ever. I turned my face away from them all, away from that world that I came to be ashamed of, ashamed not only of it because it seemed so foreign, but ashamed of myself, too, for having once been happy there. I never went back. And now I do not know where I belong.

*

She puts away the notebook with her writings and goes back to bed. When she wakes up it is evening, and she bathes and prepares dinner in an effort to regain some semblance of a normal schedule, but her head feels dull and aches. The following day is Sunday, and she follows her usual routine for the day, preparing lessons and readying her clothes for the week ahead. She even finishes hemming up the skirt that she had left undone. She does not look again at what she has written.

Monday, after school, she finds Pablito in his usual place. She is about to begin the scheduled lesson when she changes her mind. She reaches out to him and takes his hand, pulling

him out of the too-small chair. She leads him out to the playground and to the swings. She sits him in a swing and then
takes another one herself. They sit in silence for some time,
swinging gently as she looks around the school yard. The
school grounds are lovely, a green rolling field bordered by a
small stream. A far cry from her own school with its all con-
crete play-slab and chain-link fence enclosure. A far cry from
the sandy street, lime-white in the moonlight.

She begins to hum and then to sing softly the words from
the games of long ago which come to her unbidden. There is
Doña Blanca and *Naranja dulce*, where the beloved is com-
pared to a sweet orange, a song of farewell. Then there is
Hilitos de oro, about the spinner of golden threads who
refused the king his daughters. She thinks—now, as an
adult—that the games that children learned when she was a
child, and perhaps still learn today, must be of medieval origins. They were about knights saying farewell to their ladies
as they left for the wars or about rescuing the fair Lady
Blanche. Each game acted out a story, a song. Their music
had reached her once, long ago; perhaps the music will reach
Pablito now.

She stands up and pulls Pablito out of his swing in one
motion. She takes his hands again and begins walking in a
circle while she sings about rescuing Doña Blanca. Pablito
looks at her in bewilderment and then begins to laugh. She
laughs with him. When she can stop laughing she says to
him: "*Yo soy Doña Blanca. Me llamo Blanca. Blanca Estela.*"

Pablito nods his head, a knowing smile on his face. He
makes a mocking bow: "*Yo soy Pablo.* My name is Paul."

Amada Means Beloved

Many years later, even into her fifties and her sixties, Anita remembered the day they took her to meet her father. The memory stayed with her like a piece of flotsam that lay quietly beneath the water, waiting only for the right impetus to send it to the surface, where it would float briefly, and then be submerged again. She remembered the day, just like people remember what they were doing and what the weather was like when somebody died that was important to them. It was Saturday, November 3rd, in 1932.

She remembered the date because it was the day after All Souls' Day, and they had taken flowers to the little cemetery up the hill the day before. They were not real flowers, just made of paper. There was not enough water to grow flowers, so they made wreaths of pink and green tissue paper bought from the store in Jensenville. The flowers were pink, and the leaves, of course, green. She remembered what a lovely wreath she and her aunt Matilde had made. Then Matilde and Rigo, her husband, had taken it up to the cemetery. Anita stayed at home; she had to stay with the little ones, Juanito and Perlita, who were still babies and could not walk up the hill. Juanito, the oldest, was three, and Perlita had just turned two. She knew they were her cousins, but she thought of them as her little brother and sister, even as her own babies.

Anita knew it was Saturday because she was waiting for her uncle David to get off work in Jensenville and come home to pick her up and take her to the fair in town. He would drive her to town. He was so proud of the old battered car he had just bought, which was much better and faster than the mule-drawn wagon that was his vehicle before.

That day in November, Anita waited for her uncle David in front of the house, sitting on the porch steps. She had washed her hands and her face, combed her hair and put on the white dress that she had worn for her First Communion. Of course, it was short and tight since the ceremony was three years earlier. They were going to the fair, her uncle had told her. She had never been to one before, and he had tried to explain what it was—people buying and selling things, food and drink, prizes for games, carrousels and ferris wheels. She tried to imagine it all and although the possibilities seemed limitless, she could not imagine it.

Anita remembered the weather that day. It was not yet cold, but there was a chill in the air, and a slight wind kept whipping up the dust and the brown leaves that were beginning to fall. She hoped her uncle would come soon, for she was sitting in the shade, and she felt a little cold. She also hoped that he would be in a good mood, although the last weeks he had been happy again, like he used to be before Marieta went away. He told Anita that he had a girlfriend who was very nice and sweet to him, and that was why he was laughing and singing again.

She knew who David's girlfriend was. She was Lucía Rodríguez, the daughter of Don Onofre Rodríguez, who had a dairy. Lucía was the youngest of four girls. Anita knew her because Lucía had worked in the school. When Miss Yates came to teach them in English in the fourth grade, and she couldn't tell what the children were saying, she got Lucía to come and help her, to tell her what the students were saying.

Anita liked learning English. She used to sit quietly at her desk and watch Miss Yates' mouth as she formed those strange sounds. After a while she began to recognize the words, and eventually she began to learn what they meant. Then she wanted to read the books on Miss Yates' desk. There had not been many books on Miss Hinojosa's desk when she taught them the first three grades in Spanish, but she had taught them to read and write by writing words on the blackboard. When Anita was in Miss Yates' class, Miss Hinojosa got sick and had to go away. Someone had said she was consumptive, but Anita was not sure what that meant.

School ended for Anita just as she finished her first year with Miss Yates. That was after Mamá Amadita died and Marieta went away and left David and the children behind. Every time she thought of Mamá Amadita, her chest tightened and her eyes filled with tears, which embarrassed her enormously if anyone else was around. She did not remember Mamá Amadita dying, though. They told her later that when the women who dressed the body went to put Mamá Amadita in the coffin, Anita started screaming that they couldn't put her in there, how was she going to breathe, that Mamá Amadita didn't like closed places. Then they told her she fainted and lay in bed for three days, not moving, not eating until one of Mamá Amadita's old friends, Doña Petra, came in and started whipping her on the legs with a leather belt. Then she started crying, and they could comfort her.

David had decided then that he and his new wife would come and live in the house and take care of the animals—they had two milk cows, a pig and a dozen chickens—and of Anita. So David and Marieta moved in. Marieta was very beautiful, but even Anita could tell she wasn't happy. She was used to living in town, where her mother kept a boarding house, and hated being buried in the country, as she always said. She cried when she tore her stockings or her skirts as she walked through the brush to look for the eggs the hens hid. She hated having to get the water from the cistern early in the morning, and she would never learn to milk the cows. She also ruined her shoes walking through the mud to feed the pigs in the sty. Soon she was pregnant, though, and all those chores were Anita's again.

Anita liked Marieta. The young woman was always kind to her, although in an absent-minded way, as if her thoughts were somewhere else. When Anita herself got married and had to live at first with her mother-in-law, she realized that it must not have been easy for Marieta to start her married life with a seven-year-old already in place, as it were. The memory had dimmed, but years later she still remembered Marieta as having curly black hair and green eyes that were a little prominent, making her look perpetually surprised.

David was very much in love with his wife and Marieta with him, but she was also a little jealous at first, wondering if Anita was his daughter and asking whose picture it was that stood in a gilded frame on the dresser. The picture showed a smiling girl, also with curly hair, the curls held back by a hair band worn low on the forehead, and light colored eyes.

"It's Mamá Amadita," Anita had answered.

"That's right, it's Amadita," David had confirmed. Marieta looked surprised—or maybe not.

Anita grew up with that picture, and she remembered, when she was very young, pointing at it and asking Papá Juanito who it was. He took the picture from her hands and looked at it, smiling.

"It's Amadita," he answered then, too.

Anita looked from the picture to Mamá Amadita in the kitchen, at the wrinkles creasing her pale face and the gray hair pulled back tightly in a bun at the nape of her neck. The only similarity was the eyes. Mamá Amadita's eyes were pale blue and so were the girl's, for they looked pale in the photograph. And so Anita told herself: that was what Mamá Amadita looked like before I met her.

Now she waited to go to town. She had shut the front door of the house to keep out the dust; she had fed and shut up the chickens, and Juanito and Perlita were already gone for the day. Nina and José, their closest neighbors, had come in their wagon with their four children and picked them up. Nina and José did not seem old, even to Anita's young eyes. They were a very jolly couple, always laughing and joking, and they had four little children at every stage, from crawling to running. Anita heard David asking them to look after the little ones so he could take Anita to town. Nina was sitting at the kitchen table, holding a basket of eggs, because sometimes their hens wouldn't lay and they had to get some from Anita. They always tried to pay for them, but David always refused the money. This time he had asked Nina if, as a favor, they would take the little ones for the afternoon of the coming Saturday. He was going to town so Anita might see part of the fair.

"The poor girl never goes anywhere. Ever since she had to leave school, she doesn't even see kids her own age, and she's never been to a fair. Besides, I thought I might take her to see her father. She hasn't seen him for years. I don't even know if she remembers him." Nina had nodded, her smiling face serious for a moment, and agreed to do as he asked.

When Nina left, David turned to Anita, who was standing in the doorway, and said to her, "You heard what I said. Get ready to go to town on Saturday. We're going to the fair. Maybe we'll see your father, too. I don't know if you remember him." Anita nodded silently. She and David never said much. He was always too tired when he came home at night to do more than eat supper and hug the children before falling asleep. Anita felt more comfortable in silence, too. Sometimes, when she thought she had said something, she realized it was only her thoughts that had sounded so loud inside her head. This time, if she had said something, she would have told her uncle that she did, indeed, remember her father.

There was another photograph, this one in the dresser drawer, of a gray-haired couple. It was Mamá Amadita—that, she knew, without a doubt—and a man stood beside her, holding a cowboy hat in his hands. She could make out in the picture the bright black eyes, the long moustache, even the cleft of his chin. That was Papá Juanito. She remembered him, or perhaps she had an impression of him, not so much anything she remembered seeing, but rather the clinking of spurs as he came in the house and, above all, a smell. When she was grown, she realized what it was, a mixture of leather and sweat, of both man and horse. She remembered smelling it as he picked her up and perched her on the saddle of the big palomino that he always rode and that she never saw again, just as she had not seen Papá Juanito again. She might have said these things to David, but somehow, there did not seem to be a need to do so.

She could see the cloud of dust in the distance before she heard the sound of the engine or finally saw the car approaching the house. It came to a stop a few yards from where she was. David shouted, asking her if she had shut both doors. She shook her head and replied, as she walked towards him, that she had only latched the screen door in the back, and he nodded, satisfied. The two-room frame house stood on a little knoll, facing north, from where the wind was blowing. To close both doors meant, even at this time of the year, that it would be hot and stuffy when they returned; but leaving the front door open meant dust even in the bed clothes.

Anita got in the car and sat gingerly, for this was only the second time she rode in it, and she was afraid of causing the slightest damage to the miraculous vehicle that David had brought home a month earlier. They drove away, trailing a cloud of dust again. The road was only a narrow dirt track, pitted with holes. The mesquite branches whipped against the car as they went by. This was brush country. The trees that afforded shade were scarce, only an occasional huisache, not much to look at, but, oh, the wonderful fragrance it gave out with its tiny yellow flowers.

Before the road curved south in the direction of Jensenville, Anita could see the chimney top of Nina and José's house, and she wondered anxiously what the children were doing and if they were all right. She was not used to leaving them behind. Further down the road to Jensenville, they passed the dairy belonging to the Rodríguez family, and Anita thought for a minute that they would stop to take Lucía with them, but they drove on and soon approached the school where Anita had attended those four years that now seemed so long ago. She used to walk to the dairy early in the mornings and hitch a ride in the milk wagon with Don Onofre as far as the school. That stopped last year when Marieta, who had gone to town to visit her sick mother, she said, sent back word to them that she was not coming back.

Marieta ran away with one of the boarders in her mother's boarding house. Those were terrible days, with David shouting and taking out his gun, saddling his horse and flying to town. Nina came and took Anita and the little ones to her house, which was now so crowded that José had to sleep on the porch. Doña Teresa, Marieta's mother, wouldn't stop crying, Nina said, from sorrow and shame at what her daughter had done. Also from fear of David, who kept shouting that she had better tell him where that so and so of her daughter had gone to, and that if he caught up with them, he was going to kill them both. People said that what made it worse was that the man Marieta ran away with was a Gringo. Those men had no scruples. Also, if you killed one of them, they strung you up, for sure. The man was in town only a little over a month, but he had a big, fast car in which, people said, he made trips to the border. Someone said he was a *tequilero,* a liquor smuggler. No one knew where he had come from; Doña Teresa did not even rightly know his name, she just called him Joe. What everyone knew was that the two lovers were far away by now, and David didn't even know where to start looking, so he had better forget Marieta. And so he did, eventually.

Perhaps Anita was the biggest casualty of Marieta's desertion—next to the children, who were only one and two. Anita's school days ended. She stayed home from then on to look after Juanito and Perlita and to cook and clean house for her uncle. She was only ten years old. The children cried for their mother at first, but soon Anita was "Mami" to them, and she loved them in return, even as she yearned for Miss Yates' books that she would never again have a chance to read.

They were approaching town. She knew this because of the citrus groves that stood right outside Jensenville—rows and rows of orange trees bordered by palm trees and salt cedars to break the wind. Metal pipes encircled the fields to provide precious water for irrigation.

David had not made a crop this year. Anita watched along with him as the corn withered in the sun, midget ears drying on the stalk. There were no melons or onions or squash either. David had gone to town then to look for a job. He stayed there several days with his sister Matilde while Anita stayed alone in the house with the children. She was not afraid of being alone at night, had never feared the dark, but she began to worry about food. They were down to one cow and her calf since the stock pond was almost dry, and they could not share the precious cistern water with the animals. She was grateful, though, that there was still milk for the children, even if not as much and as rich as before because there was not any grass left. The cattle were now eating mesquite pods, and David was burning cactus pears for them. They still had the chickens and, therefore, eggs to eat, some beef jerky and a little flour; but she watched the foodstuffs dwindle like the crops in the field that summer. Then David returned from town, bringing groceries with him. He had found work with Mr. Jensen in the packing sheds. They would soon be shipping oranges all over the United States, and additional men were needed. With the promise of a job, he could get credit at the grocery store. Anita felt a great weight slip from her back.

David began working for Mr. Jensen late that summer. He packed and sometimes picked onions first, and then oranges. He would leave home at dawn to hitch a ride with Don Onofre in the milk wagon, helping the old man deliver milk on the way to town in payment for the ride. David was an intelligent and hard working man, and Mr. Jensen soon made him foreman in his packing shed. With that came a little more money and then—miracle of miracles—the opportunity to buy a car.

The car was old and needed repairs, but he got it cheap when they auctioned off Fausto Garrido's property to pay his creditors. Mr. Jensen lent David the money to buy the car, and David agreed to repay the loan out of his wages, which would be deducted every month by the amount of the payment. One man's misfortune was another man's benefit, David said, looking fondly at the 1918 Model T.

First, the water tank came into view, high on its spindly legs of steel, then they passed Mr. Jensen's packing sheds and warehouses, and then they came up to Mr. Bland's feed store and gasoline pumps. Anita knew they had arrived. David waved at the men standing outside the feed store; one of them was Mr. Bland. Mr. Bland and Mr. Jensen were the richest men in town—even Anita had heard that. They next came into view of Mr. Jensen's house. It was white and had two stories, the only two-storied house in town, with pillars and verandas all around it. Anita could not understand though—any more than the other Mexicans could—why such a grand house was made of wood. Rich people's houses should be made of stone. The house was set far back from the street and seemed to contain within its white picket fence all the greenery in town—a grass lawn, shrubs and poplars, all neatly trimmed. She could not imagine the abundance of water required to keep it alive. Anita gave an involuntary "Aahh!" at the sight of such verdant luxury. David turned to look at her.

"Pedro keeps it looking very pretty, doesn't he? Mr. Jensen says he's the best gardener he ever had. That's why he didn't want to lose him. When they came to deport him, Mr. Jensen talked to Mr. Bland, who's his friend and the county judge. Mr. Bland took care of things; he talked to the *rinches*, and they let Pedro stay, as long as he works for Mr. Jensen." David called all Americans in uniform *rinches*, whether they were Rangers or customs men; everybody they knew did the same.

Anita nodded, accepting the information, although she did not know who David was talking about. Whoever it was, she was grateful to him for keeping this spot green and well tended. Looking at it gave her a sense of calm.

They drove on towards the center of town, still trailing dust behind them. Occasionally they encountered another car, and each driver would honk and wave. Anita wondered if they would perhaps see some of her classmates, and what they would think to see her riding in a car. But they did not. Instead, they passed a group of men standing outside the bus station and café. David waved at them, and they waved back. The grocery store was on the next block. The sign painted on the wall still said "Garrido General Merchandise" and underneath *Mercancías en General*. David pointed at it and said, "They will soon paint over the sign. Mr. Bland bought the store. I don't know how Fausto Garrido lasted here so long. Finally, the big fish ate him up."

Anita had never seen fish, but she thought she knew what he meant. David continued, "I don't think the bosses ever liked Fausto. They thought he put on airs—always wearing a coat and tie and driving a car." He paused and laughed, "And now I'm driving his car. But the boss likes me. He said I was a good worker."

Anita could still see Fausto Garrido, as she saw him the times she had visited his store. Always a coat, a bow tie— and a white shirt, even if his sleeves were rolled up and the coat came off when it was very hot. He was tall and thin, with light brown hair slicked back from the high forehead, golden brown eyes and a ruddy face, some said from drinking. But he always looked so clean, and he was very polite. Anita knew he did not come from these parts. She asked David once about Fausto, and he told her that Fausto Garrido came from the other side of the river soon after the Revolution, when he was practically a boy, and opened the store shortly afterwards. People said his family in Mexico had money and a big store, that they wanted to take advantage of the growth in the Valley, now that the Americans were coming from up north and started irrigated farming.

It was clear that Fausto Garrido was an educated man. He was often seen reading books, and he soon learned English and practiced speaking it with Mr. Jensen and Mr. Bland. Anita heard David and Rigo say once that it was more than English that Fausto practiced with Edna, Mr. Wright's young wife from Los Olmos. She would come into the store in high heels and wearing a hat, pink and white skin and fluffy blond hair, swinging her hips and smiling at the storekeeper, with whom she had long conversations, longer than was necessary to order flour, sugar, coffee and soap. Hardly anyone else understood what they said, but they could all see the smiles and the looks the two exchanged. And now Fausto Garrido was gone. Perhaps Mr. Wright did not like those weekly shopping trips of his wife. Perhaps the bosses did not like Fausto, as David said. Perhaps the farmers were not able to pay Fausto for what they bought from him, so he, in turn, could not pay his creditors; or perhaps he just didn't belong in this part of the Valley. So they auctioned off the merchandise in the store, his car and even the furniture in his house, and now Mr. Bland had the store and David had the car.

They finally came to some vacant lots at the other end of town, where a crowd of people were milling about. Tents had been set up, one of which advertised moving pictures inside, and, to Anita's delight, there was a carrousel of little painted wooden horses, going round and round, and an enormous wheel with seats attached precariously, also going round and round, but so high up in the air that her stomach felt funny just to look at it. David noticed her amazement and, uncharacteristically, gave her a quick hug and laughed, "You have never seen any of this before, have you?" and asked her if she wanted a ride.

"Not yet," she answered, not wanting to disappoint him by showing that she felt apprehensive.

"All right, we'll wait for your rides. Let's look around first." They walked in the crowd for a few minutes, Anita dazed by the sounds, sights and smells that surrounded her: loud voices, laughter, music from the carrousel, the girls' brightly colored dresses, the aroma of steaming corn on the cob and fresh tamales, the dust that floated like a veil over everything. Her senses had not been assaulted with such overpowering force before. She did something unlike her; she put out her hand and took David's.

They spotted Lucía Rodríguez, waving at them. She was standing by her sister, Rosa, and Rosa's husband, Artemio. They walked towards the trio. Lucía flashed a smile at David, which he returned with a frown, since he did not know what Rosa and her husband thought of his courtship of

Lucía. David knew that Don Onofre was angry with him, saying that if he had known how his kindness would be repaid, he would have never given David a ride to town in the milkwagon all those mornings. After all, David was still married, even if his wife had abandoned him; what could he offer Lucía was certainly not a proper marriage. David did not know if Rosa and Artemio were there to provide cover, to camouflage the fact that he and Lucía were together, or to ward him off. The couple seemed friendly enough though, so he attempted a smile that included all three, and Lucía reached down and gave Anita a hug.

"Well, shall we look around first," asked Artemio, a little bantam rooster of a man, much smaller and slighter than his substantial wife. "Or shall we have an ice?" But then he added, "I don't know about you, but I am tired of just standing around."

They all followed the little man's lead as he walked towards a clearing where several makeshift tables and wooden benches had been set up. A man stood by a metal cart and served scoops of shaved ice flavored with fruit syrup. Artemio insisted it was his treat, and he began by asking Anita what flavor she wanted. She chose orange. The others opted for strawberry or orange, too, and for the next few minutes no one spoke as they struggled to eat the ice before it soaked through the paper cone and started to dribble down their hands. Anita liked the sweet taste of the orange-flavored ice at first, but soon her lips and her mouth began to feel numb and her throat began to hurt.

When they were finished, Artemio exclaimed, "That was refreshing! How about some steaming hot corn now to counteract the cold, and so we don't get a sore throat?"

Rosa, who until now had not spoken, said in her monotone voice, "We'll get sick, eating all that mixture of things."

"Don't be silly, woman," her husband replied, "it all gets mixed up inside the stomach, anyway." And so they ate corn on the cob, as well.

As they stood around, nibbling on the corn, David and Artemio talked, while Rosa and Lucía carried on a whispered conversation. Anita tried to listen to all of them.

"Do you think you'll be able to hang on next year?" Artemio was asking. "This year you didn't even make a crop. Of course, nobody else did, unless they had irrigation, and only the Gringos have the money for that. But how long can you go on—going back and forth to town every day, the expense of gasoline and all, and this little girl left alone all day with the babies? What if something happens to them?"

David nodded his head. "I know, I know. I lie awake at night, wondering what is going to happen to us all. Without irrigation we're doomed. But it's not just up to me—selling out, I mean. You know the ranch is not mine only. It also belongs to my sisters, and to Anita," he added, surprised. "I keep forgetting about her like that. She's more like my own. For that reason I can't just walk away from the land; you know what happens when you do that. Before you know it, someone moves your fences, and you have nothing left. And as to selling, I don't want to do that, even though I know Mr. Jensen has been buying tracts close to me. But, anyway, if I wanted to sell it, it's not just up to me."

Anita was surprised. She had not heard David speak so much at one time before.

"You are right," Artemio stated seriously. "One should never sell land. Not that you would have to worry about your sisters interfering with what you want to do. They understand that you do what you have to do."

Artemio changed the subject to complain about his father-in-law. "He is such a mean-tempered old man. He needs help with the dairy, and he lets me do the work, all right, but I can't make the slightest suggestion that he doesn't start yelling about the good-for-nothings his daughters married, who can't wait for him to die to grab everything. And you know I'm the only one who does anything for him. The others, my brothers-in-law, don't care if he drops dead. I didn't marry Rosa for her property, I've got land of my own . . ."

Anita knew Artemio had land, but not much. Everyone in the area (except perhaps the Americans, who were newcomers), even those as young as Anita, knew the family histories of the others around them. They recited genealogies like they recited the rosary at wakes and funerals. At every gathering there would be stories of who had married whom and how many children they had and what land was theirs. There had been only a few families who had settled in this harsh and isolated country, encouraged by grants of land from the King of Spain. But the families had many children, and the lands were divided and subdivided until each descendant claimed only ten or twenty acres, and how could anyone live on that.

Then the Americans came, and one way or another, the land began passing into their hands. Towns like Jensenville, named after people that were still alive, were created out of old *ranchos* or river crossings. Now they taught you in school that people like Mr. Jensen brought civilization to this forsaken land.

David and Artemio went on talking, Lucía and Rosa continued to whisper, but Anita was no longer listening. Her eyes were drawn to the tent where light and shadows projected grotesque silhouettes against the canvas. She had seen a moving picture only once before, and it enthralled her. She wondered whether she would have the courage to ask David to let her go into the tent, whether he could give her the admission fee. She noticed only then that the four adults had fallen silent. She looked inquiringly at her uncle and then followed the direction of his gaze.

A few feet away from them stood a man. He was tall and thin, with stooped shoulders and surprisingly large, strong hands that clutched a straw hat. She did not know why she was reluctant to look at his face. It was only when David said, "Good evening, Pedro, how are you?" that she looked up and saw, with a shudder, that he was looking at her. He had thick, black hair, streaked with gray, that fell across his forehead and a long, thin face, with a scar running down his cheek. But what frightened her most were his dark eyes which were the same as hers. She gave a little gasp, which no one heard as David asked, "Come on, girl, aren't you going to say anything to your father?"

She stood completely still and silent until the pressure of David's hand on her back, pushing her forward, became unbearable. "That is not Papá Juanito," she cried out and bolted away running across the fair grounds, bumping into people who looked at her in surprise. The lights, the music and the laughter now mocked her and magnified the misery of suddenly not knowing where she belonged.

They found her about thirty minutes later, huddled behind a stack of folding chairs outside the movie tent. "It's all right," David said, putting his arm around her, "We're going home."

On the way back, Lucía rode in the car with them, Anita sitting in the middle, fast asleep, with her head resting on the young woman's shoulder. They stopped just before they got to the dairy and waited for Rosa and Artemio to catch up with them. When they did, Lucía got out of the car and joined them, and they all said good night. Anita was awake now, but David did not say anything. He was not angry, he just seemed a little puzzled, shaking his head once in a while. They went and picked up the children, who were already asleep and who promptly started crying when they were awakened. Anita was busy the next hour or so, putting the children to bed and waiting for them to go back to sleep. And finally she, too, went to sleep.

They did not speak of her father again, and their lives went on as before. About a year later, Don Onofre García died, and Lucía eloped with David. They called it an elopement, but it was more of a premeditated move. Doña Engracia, Don Onofre's widow, felt that out of deference to her dead husband's views, she could not condone the proposed cohabitation of her daughter with a man who was still married to another in the eyes of the law, even if, perhaps, God was more understanding or more forgiving. She, therefore, turned a blind eye to the elaborate preparations for the elopement.

Lucía thus came to live with them. Anita grew to love her quickly. She did not have the beauty nor the vague air of mystery that had surrounded Marieta, but she was kind and loving. Within the year, Lucía gave birth to a baby boy, and David began to work on adding a room to the house. Anita thought the baby was the most beautiful she had ever seen, and there began a struggle with her conscience as to whether by loving this baby she was slighting Juanito and Perlita. Soon after the birth of Lucía's baby, Matilde and Rigo's youngest child died. She was a girl of fourteen who never grew or developed but remained an infant instead, always requiring care. It was because she had to look after this child that Matilde had not been able to take in Anita after Mamá Amadita's death. Now Matilde decided that Anita should come to live with them in town, and she and Rigo came one day to the ranch house to take Anita back with them. Anita was almost thirteen.

Anita was happy living with her aunt and uncle, but she missed the children at first. She had been a mother before she had been a child, she reflected years later. The sense of responsibility and seriousness that was thrust on her at such a young age never left her. Sometimes a fleeting regret crossed her thoughts: if she had lived with Matilde when she was younger, she might have stayed in school longer. But that thought soon vanished as she reminded herself that she would not have had the two little ones for those years.

David and Lucía went on to have five children in all, in addition to the two from his marriage to Marieta. Anita loved them all, but not with the same all-consuming fervor of her childhood. And, Anita soon went on to marry and have her own children. When she was seventeen, she married Leo Hernández, a gentle and kind young man from Los Olmos. They did not have money for a house of their own, so Anita and Leo lived with his parents and a younger sister for the first three years of their marriage. Anita was not happy with the situation; she wanted her own home, especially after the babies came—two in the first three years. But she put on a good face and hoped for change. It came in early 1941 when Leo's older brother, who was working in

San Antonio, wrote to him, telling him of the work to be found there. Leo knew the limited opportunities that he faced where he was—working for Mr. Jensen, or for Mr. Bland, or for Mr. Wright or for whichever Anglo patrón there was. And so, they moved to San Antonio. The war came, and Leo and his brother and all the young men they knew joined the armed forces. Afterwards, some came back to pick up their lives where they had left off or to make new ones, but some did not come back at all. Leo, however, came back well and in one piece, and they had four more children and made for themselves a better life than they had thought possible back in Los Olmos or Jensenville.

But she did not forget the brush country and the life there, just as she did not forget her kindly aunt Matilde, who had given her, when at last she had asked for it, that part of her history that had been missing. On the day before they were to leave for San Antonio, Anita paid her aunt a visit to say goodbye. And, as she was leaving, Anita finally asked, "Where did my father come from?"

Matilde told her the story of how Pedro Alfaro, a fugitive from the blood-bath of the Mexican Revolution, was washed up, literally, by the Rio Grande onto its banks, "on this side." He was sick and weak and had a big gash on his face, down the cheek. Several people had befriended him and given him food and shelter, including Papá Juanito and Mamá Amadita. When he was well, Pedro Alfaro went to town and worked doing odd jobs for Mr. Jensen since he was not strong enough to do field work. Mr. Jensen found out that Pedro liked working with garden plants and had a great talent for it, and that was what he put him to doing.

The people of Jensenville and of the *ranchos* accepted Pedro Alfaro and soon paid little attention to him. Pedro Alfaro, in the meantime, had fallen in love with Amadita, the youngest child, the pride and joy of Don Juan Guerra and Doña Amada de los Santos, his wife. Amadita was born when her mother was over forty. She arrived six years after her closest brother, David, and after three miscarriages and a stillbirth. Amadita took after her mother, had the same dark gold hair, the same blue eyes that only appeared in the Santos family in one out of six or seven children. Both the parents and the other children adored her; she was the pretty one in the family, the only blonde and blue-eyed child. And when she was seventeen, Pedro Alfaro wanted to marry her. He came and spoke to her parents one Sunday, and he was given a resounding no for an answer and told not to come back again. They might be poor, but they knew who they were. Who was he? He told them.

Pedro had been a young school teacher in his native border state of Coahuila when, in 1914, he joined the rebels that had risen against the tyrant who had seized the Presidency of Mexico through a bloody treason. For four years he followed the rebel armies, as a foot soldier first, but then, when his commanding officer learned that Pedro had been a teacher, they used him mainly as a scribe, drafting letters and dispatches and reading incoming correspondence, so scarce were the men who could read and write. Then came the terrible time of betrayals and assassinations. Pedro's unit was defeated, and he was taken prisoner. He eventually escaped from the enemy camp and fled, following the river south, looking perhaps for the place where the Rio Grande empties into the Gulf of Mexico and, when he was almost there, finally crossed the river. He did not know why he had not crossed it before. Perhaps he wanted to put off that final step as long as possible.

Amadita's family was not impressed. He was still a foreigner to them, and Doña Amada would not hear of the marriage. Pedro and Amadita waited for more than a year, and then Pedro went to his boss, Mr. Jensen, and told him of his predicament. With the cold logic of the Americans, Mr. Jensen asked Pedro several questions, including the girl's age. Pedro told him. "Well, she is of age," Mr. Jensen said, "and does not need her parents' consent. You can be married in the courthouse." And so they were, Amadita having first practiced elaborate deceit by telling her parents that she was going to town to visit some friends.

Amadita's action almost killed her parents with grief,

especially her mother. They did not see her or speak to her again until they found out that she was about to have a baby. Amadita and Pedro were living in town, and Doña Amada arrived at their two-room house as Amadita was going into labor. She stayed there until a baby girl was born, many hours later, and was still there when her daughter first became feverish, then delirious, and later on when she died.

Doña Amada allowed Pedro to see his daughter only once and granted him the wish that she should be named Ana, after his mother. Then she took the child to raise as her own, although she was nearly an old woman by then.

Anita packed the photographs of her mother and of her grandparents in a little cedar chest and took them to her new home in San Antonio. She packed away, together with the photographs, the memory of her father and of that evening in November when her world had changed so suddenly, but every so often the memories would escape the cedar chest and come troubling her with questions. When she found it difficult to read the letters Leo Jr. wrote during his Army service, she cried angrily to herself, "Why, if my father was a school teacher, did he let me go almost illiterate?" When her first daughter was born, and Leo wanted to name her Amada, she refused without knowing why, only saying, "Two Amadas are enough. After all, why was I not named Amada, like my mother?" She added to herself, "Perhaps I was not loved enough by anyone." When her children asked about their grandparents on their mother's side, she told them curtly that her mother had died while having her, and her father had abandoned her.

One day, when her Tía Matilde was quite old, and Anita's two youngest children were already in high school, a letter came for Anita from Jensenville. In it her aunt told Anita that her father, Pedro Alfaro, was very sick and close to death, and perhaps she might want to see him. She thought about it for several days without saying anything to anyone and finally told Leo that she was going to see her father in Jensenville, alone.

Tía Matilde met her at the bus station and took her home with her. The next day, she took Anita to the house where her father lived. It was a four-room frame house in need of paint, but it had the prettiest little garden in front, with rows of brightly colored zinnias and marigolds flanking the high wooden porch. He had remarried, and his wife, younger than he, was a quiet, pleasant faced woman, who greeted them courteously. Anita's aunt and stepmother stayed in the front room while she walked timidly into the bedroom to see the man she had not seen in more than thirty years.

He lay still on the bed, his breath so slight it hardly stirred the bedcovers. Anita did not say anything, she merely sat in the chair next to the bed. She did not know how long she sat there. She could hear the murmur of the two women's voices in the front room, but all was silent in the bedroom. The sick man finally stirred with something like a tremor, and he turned his head and looked at her. She saw again, with shock, her own eyes looking back at her from the sunken face where the scar still stood out like a livid welt. He whispered something, and she leaned forward to catch what he said. He repeated the whisper, and she thought he said, "Amada."

She shook her head and said, "No. Ana. Anita. Your daughter." She thought she saw him smile, but it may have been a grimace, for he seemed to be in pain. He closed his eyes and said nothing more, but then she saw a tear coursing slowly down his cheek. Almost involuntarily, she put out her hand and put it over his. She did not know how long she sat there with his hand in hers. He seemed to have fallen asleep. The room was already in shadows when she heard her aunt call from the door, "It's late, Anita. You can came back tomorrow."

They said goodbye to Pedro's wife and thanked her for letting them visit him. She replied courteously that they were welcome any time, this was their home. "Your father's home is your own," she added to Anita. "Please come back whenever you want to, for as long as you want to. You will come tomorrow?" Anita told her she would.

He died that night, and he was buried the day after in the old Mexican cemetery in Jensenville. His first wife lay in the little cemetery on the sandy hill, a short walk from the ranch house, that Anita remembered visiting as a child, but that land was all now owned by Mr. Jensen or his successors. They had respected those graves, but nobody else could be buried there any more.

After the funeral, Tía Matilde saw her off at the bus station. Anita kissed the old woman and felt in that frail embrace all the love that had never needed words. On the long ride back, as she looked out at the harsh, monotonous landscape, she thought of Matilde and of Rigo, who was now dead, of David and Lucía, who now lived in Corpus Christi, of Papá Juanito and Mamá Amadita, lying in the small cemetery on the hill, next to their darling Amadita. Had her grandparents ever loved her as much as they had loved their own daughter? Had they ever blamed Anita for her death? Was that really why she had not been called Amada? And what about her father, that poor man who had lost both wife and daughter almost at the same time. Had he loved her? She remembered the paper-thin touch of his hand as he lay in bed and the tear rolling down his cheek. She remembered Mr. Jensen's verdant garden and the brightly colored row of zinnias.

"What can I tell my children about their grandparents?" she wondered. She thought about it for some time; then she came to a decision. "I can tell them that their grandparents loved each other so much that they defied great opposition in order to get married. That they were happy while they were together." She was sure of that. And for herself, she added, "I can tell them that I, too, was loved, even if I was not called *Amada*."

Margarita

Margo had always hated the time and place in which she was born. She did not really wish she had been born someone else since she had a warm, affectionate family of whom she was truly fond, but if she could have transported them all to Paris or New York, or if they could have all lived in fifteenth-century Spain, or been French or Anglo-Saxon whenever, she would have been happy. But to have been born in South Texas, to live in Texas in 1964, in the shadow of the Alamo—both the building and the movie—as a Mexican, that was to be one of fortune's stepchildren.

She was born Margarita Ancira, twenty years earlier, in Los Encinos, Texas, population 3,000, a place as dry and dusty as only a small town in South Texas can be. Hot for at least nine months out of the year, bitterly cold for perhaps two weeks in the winter, and always gray. Gray blowing dust, gray thorny brush that belied the town's name, since not a solitary oak was to be found. Except for the sky; the sky was always blue. The horizon in Los Encinos was infinite, and that limitless expanse of blue crushed Margo with a sense of desolation. Margo would pray for rain, as did her father, but for different reasons. Rain, mist, fog, would have blurred the horizon, broken the monotony, but the rain, like change, seldom came.

At the moment Margo also hated the time and place she was in, although she was not in Los Encinos. She was in the library of the University of Texas at 7:30 on a June evening, too late to find a place at a study table. She circled around the room in a miserable mood, hating herself for arriving late, hating herself for being at the University of

Texas at all. She felt so adventuresome, enrolling for the summer session at the big university, instead of spending the summer with her family at Los Encinos. They were hurt that she had not chosen to be with them for the summer after having spent the spring in Europe, studying in Madrid and traveling through Spain and France with a dozen other girls from Sacred Heart College in San Antonio, where she would be a senior in the fall.

Margo had the notion when she enrolled for the summer session that she would perhaps transfer to the university in the fall for good. She felt she was ready for a big coed school, where the students came from all parts of the state, even from all parts of the country, and even from abroad. She had become impatient with Sacred Heart, a school so much like home, where her friendships were confined to nice, Catholic girls, mainly from South Texas and northern Mexico, her dates circumscribed by the limits of her classmates' male relations, all nice Catholic boys. How she wished now, as she looked at the blank stares and indifferent faces, that she was back home, relating her European experiences to her family and making plans to return to Sacred Heart in the fall.

She thought she saw a vacant place at a table for two at the back of the room. She hurried towards it; she *must* find a place to study for her test on Milton tomorrow. She arrived, almost breathless in her hurry, and set down her books in front of the empty chair, across from a bowed blond head. Eyes as blue and as cold as a mountain lake looked into hers as the occupant raised his head and said curtly: "That place is taken."

Margo felt her face grow hot, and she knew it must be glowing red. She stood immobile for a second or two. Perhaps he noticed her embarrassment because he added, "Sorry," but as an afterthought.

She clutched her books to her chest as if they could shield her from rebuffs and hurried away from the table and out of the room. She was so stupid, so incredibly stupid, she lashed out at herself. Two weeks she had been in this place, and she had not made a single friend, why did she ever come here? People didn't give her the time of day; they walked past her on the street, on the campus, as though she wasn't there. And now they wouldn't even let her sit at a library table.

She had not even made friends with her roommate, who was never in the room. Perhaps that was a good thing now. She could go back to her room and study, safe in the knowledge that she would be alone and without interruptions. But something in her balked at this solution. It was like falling off a horse; you had to get back on it again. If she went back to her room now, she knew that she would not dare come back to the library tomorrow, and she would end up being a prisoner in her room, afraid to go out and risk any more rebuffs like tonight's. She walked up the stairs to the next floor and circled that room till she came to a table with a couple on one side and a girl on the other, next to an empty chair. She set down her books and pulled out the chair, almost defiantly. Nobody looked up or even gave a sign that they noticed her. She sat down, opened her book, and read Milton.

She was back at the dorm by ten, amply making curfew, and had already showered and was in her nightclothes when her roommate came rushing in, muttering about how the old hag of the housemother almost locked her out. Margo's roommate had a hectic social life, was seldom in for meals, sometimes checking out for the evening, and had, so far, been away every weekend. Margo, however, did not know what her roommate did, or where she went, or if she ever went to class. Her name was Consuelo, and, though she was friendly to Margo, she was never in long enough for Margo to have learned anything about her.

When Margo first arrived at the dorm, before the summer session started, she found the two names posted on the door to the room: "Consuelo and Margo." She had groaned to herself, "Consuelo—another girl from back home. Will I never meet anybody else?" But Consuelo Wolf was not from back home, that much Margo had learned almost immediately. Consuelo was tall, between five-ten and five-eleven, and slender, with beautiful pale white skin, jet black hair, worn piled up high on her head, and enormous blue eyes, fringed by dark eyelashes and black eyeliner.

No, Consuelo was nothing like the girls she had grown up with in Los Encinos, nor like Teresita, her roommate at Sacred Heart. Teresita was from the border, plump and friendly, and with those remnants of tomboyishness that Margo had come to associate with girls who had attended convent school since childhood. Teresita was not pretty or glamorous by any means, but Margo envied her, nonetheless. She envied Teresita's complete unselfconsciousness and self-assurance. Whether a girl—or even a boy—was from Texas or Tennessee, whether the name was Smith or Sánchez, it was all the same to Teresita. Of course, Teresita's family was well off, being in the import-export business in Laredo, as well as having land, which, no doubt, went a long way to making her self-assured; but Margo's family was not so different from Teresita's in that respect.

Margo's mother's family, the large García clan, still held on to the lands of their forefathers, and of others' forefathers, who had been imprudent or profligate. The Garcías were boisterous, aggressive, and the shrewdest cattlemen and traders. Margo's father, Rafael Ancira, was a quiet man, in contrast to his wife's family, with a good head for accounting and business. Unlike his wife and her family, whose roots went back some two hundred years in Texas, he was a relative newcomer, having arrived from Mexico in 1930 as a young man of eighteen, penniless but with a good education. The young Rafael had gone to work as a clerk in his future father-in-law's feed store and had eventually married the daughter of the family. He had stayed on in Los Encinos where, together with his wife's brothers, he soon acquired the local cattle auction house, which, in addition to the feed store and the cattle, made them all a comfortable living and paid Margo's college tuition and European trip without any hardship. Yet, with all this, Margo hated what she was, or what people thought she was—a Mexican in Texas. Born and bred in the place, with a pedigree longer than the life of the state, but still an outsider.

The following evening found Margo at the library before seven. She had hurried through dinner to make sure she would find a place to study on the second floor of the library, which, for some reason, suited her better than the others. It was an attempt, she realized, to make something familiar and more her own if she went to the same spot every evening. Tonight it was the French Symbolists that she had to read, and she set about doing so with the minimum use of the dictionary. To her gratified surprise, she was able to read the poetry almost fluently and with enjoyment. At nine, she allowed herself a break, first spreading out her books as a sign of possession, lest someone think the place had been vacated. "What a place," she thought, "you spend all your waking hours fighting just to keep what you have."

She went out in the lobby to smoke a cigarette. She had taken up smoking that spring in Europe, not because she particularly enjoyed it, but because it gave one something to do with the hands. Better than standing about with arms hanging limply at the sides. She allowed herself only one cigarette per break and was almost at the end of it when the rude acquaintance from the previous evening approached the bench she was sitting on, apparently to use the same standing ashtray she was using. He did not seem to recognize her, and she looked down, busying herself in stubbing out her cigarette. As she reached for her handbag in preparation for leaving, she looked up and noticed that he was staring at her with a puzzled expression. "Don't I know you from somewhere?" he asked.

She felt her face grow hot again, but, as her grandmother would say, the blood of the Garcías showed through, and her embarrassment turned to anger.

"I don't know. Do I know *you*?"

"I'm sorry. I guess that sounded rude. It's just that I thought I had met you somewhere. Maybe from a class. My name is Mike," he continued, oblivious to the fact that she stood, handbag over her shoulder, in a pose of arrested departure.

"No, I don't think we have any classes together. I'm only taking two, and I'm new here."

"Oh, where did you transfer from? Or, are you a freshman?"

"I'm here for summer school; I don't know if I'll transfer. I'm a junior, will be a senior next fall."

He looked at her expectantly, waiting for her to finish furnishing the information requested, and she found that politeness demanded that she do so. "The reason we are always at a disadvantage with the Gringos," she had heard her father say once with exasperation, "is that we were brought up to be polite. They always take advantage of that." Margo understood now what her father meant.

"I came here from Sacred Heart in San Antonio," she finally said, as she started to walk away.

"Wait, how about going out to get some coffee?" She noticed that people at the university always said they were going for coffee, even if they drank Cokes.

She shook her head, "I've got a report due tomorrow."

"Okay, how about tomorrow? I'll meet you here at nine-thirty." She was beginning to shake her head again when he added, "All right, I've just realized it was you I was rude to last night. I'm sorry. I was having a hard time with my chemistry, and I had promised to save a seat for a friend. But I am sorry."

Politeness was truly her undoing, she thought, but how to refuse an apology. She smiled, "Fine. Nine-thirty," and started to walk away for the second time.

"Wait," he said. "What's your name?"

"Margo," and this time she left.

She arrived at nine-thirty-five, and he was already waiting. During the day she had told herself he would probably not show up, but if he did appear, she would go to the student union with him or at most to the coffee shop across the street from the campus, nowhere else. She did not know him; she did not know the city. Her mother's warnings about picking up strange men came echoing back. He suggested the coffee shop across the street, saying only oddballs frequented the union at this time of evening. It was fine with her.

He got coffee for both of them, and they sat at a booth at the back of the long room. At this time of the evening the place was still fairly full, but nothing like in the mornings when all the tables were crowded with large, noisy groups from the sororities and fraternities who excluded anyone else, as Margo had found out the first week of school.

He sat across from her and suddenly smiled at her. It was as if a bright light had illuminated his face from within, she noticed, with a tightening at her throat. A mirror on the opposite wall reflected them both. He was not so different from her. They were both slender, the same delicate bones—too delicate for him, perhaps?—the same fine mouth and straight nose. His eyes were clear blue, though, transparent as the mountain lakes she had been reminded of before, his hair a pale blond, where both eyes and hair were a rich brown in her, his skin of the fairness that burns rather than tans, while hers was already a warm gold. The differences were obviously greater than the similarities, she concluded.

"And now tell me all about yourself. Why are you here, what is your major, what do you want to do?"

She told him again about going to Sacred Heart, and she thought for a moment that he was going to give her that knowing smile she sometimes got from non-Catholic boys when she told them that she attended a Catholic girls college. One air force lieutenant she had gone out with in San Antonio—her one Anglo date—had kept asking her if the nuns really shaved their heads and if Catholic school girls were really as wild as people said. This time there were no questions about the nuns, so she told him, instead, that she had a double major in French and Spanish and a minor in English, and that she would probably end up being a teacher, although perhaps she might be a translator or an interpreter.

He told her his name was Mike Anderson, and he was a pre-med major. His father was a doctor, and he had two younger sisters. What a coincidence, she had two younger brothers. He was having a hard time with organic chemistry.

She had never taken it, never would, if she could help it. What was her last name? Margo's heart sank to her stomach at the question that had ended friendships before. There was no sense in muttering it; she would only have to repeat it. She would not disguise it with an English-sounding pronunciation; she had too much pride for that.

"Ancira," she said clearly. It was not a common name.

"Ancira," he repeated, but not sounding like her. "Is that Italian or Spanish?"

"Spanish."

"Are you Spanish?"

Margo winced at the euphemism. In Texas there were no Spaniards, or very few, but people thought they were sparing your feelings if they called you Spanish instead of Mexican. Margo's father understood the sentiment behind the words (although they only considered your feelings if your skin was light), but he always set them straight. "No," Don Rafael would say courteously, "we have been in the New World some three or four hundred years, even longer, we have Indian blood; Spain was too long ago." But Margo was not made of the same stuff as her father, so when asked if she was Spanish, she said, "Yes."

Mike's family lived on the Gulf Coast, just outside Corpus Christi, and he had never been to Los Encinos, although he knew that it was about a hundred miles away from Corpus Christi. What a coincidence, both of them being from South Texas. Mike's grandparents had come to South Texas in the 1920's and had started farming irrigated land. His mother, though, was born in Minnesota, where the older Andersons had come from originally.

Mike talked and Margo listened to him, superimposing on his face that of another boy named Mike she had met in her senior year in high school. His name was Mike Perkins, and he had had a round, friendly face that freckled in the sun. Blond hair and blue eyes too. Mike Perkins had come to Los Encinos his senior year in high school. His father worked for the oil company that had a big field near Los Encinos. Because the family moved often, Mike had gone to three different high schools. They were, what Margo's father called, itinerants.

That Mike had not known how things stood in Los Encinos. He had asked Margo to help him in geometry class and, then to repay her the favor, he had asked her to go for a Coke with him and his friends after school. Mike's friends of course, were the Anglo kids from whom came the football captain and the homecoming queen, the ones that, although in the minority, ran things in the school, just as their parents did in the town and in the county. Margo had gone with them to the Dairy Queen for a Coke, and they were not unfriendly to her, but she could see the raised eyebrows. Margo's friends, too, had asked themselves what she was doing with the Gringos.

She looked at her watch. It was ten-twenty, four years later. She needed to rush to make curfew by ten-thirty. She thanked Mike for the coffee and said she must run. He protested that they had to continue their conversation, and said he would meet her again the following evening, same place, same time.

He did, and they went back to the same table and resumed the conversation from the night before. He told her his father was an obstetrician and had delivered thousands of babies in South Texas. He did a lot of charity work among the Mexicans. Mike, as the only son, was expected to follow in his father's footsteps. But Mike wasn't sure he wanted his father's life—out at all hours, seldom having a meal or an evening at home.

She told him about her father, a quiet, courtly man, who seemed out of place in the rough cattle country. He had come to Texas in 1930, during the strife that had erupted between the Mexican government and the Catholic Church. Her father had been a young seminarian, not quite eighteen years old, but active in protesting anticlerical government policies. He had to flee the country, fearing for his life. He took the wrong train out of Monterrey and ended up in rural South Texas, instead of in San Antonio, where he had intended to go.

Mike seemed fascinated. Her father was a priest! No, no, she corrected him. Her father had never been a priest. He was studying to be a priest, but he had to drop out of the seminary. He had never taken any vows. That explained why Margo went to Catholic school; her family must be very religious. Not particularly, she told him. They went to church on Sunday and kept the major holy days, but that was not the reason she attended Sacred Heart. It was only with the Sisters that her parents would allow her to live away from home. It had been very difficult to convince them to let her come to Austin for summer school. Even here she was supposed to stay at the Catholic dorm, but it was full. It was not so much a question of being religious as it was of being a proper, well-brought up young lady. Not like the Americans, as her mother would say, who are ill-bred and immoral. But she did not say this. It would not have been polite.

The conversation ended, again, with her impending curfew, but this time he walked with her back to her dorm. The dorm was actually a large privately owned boarding house that prided itself in the personal attention and genteel atmosphere it offered girls. It was not inexpensive, but the food was good and the maid service prompt. Mike remarked that he knew a girl who lived in Margo's dorm, and she asked him who it was, but the name meant nothing to her. It turned out that the girl was away for the summer, anyway. She felt a pang of wistfulness and envy. Who was he when he was among his friends, in his own environment and not in isolation, as she knew him? It must be wonderful, she thought, to belong in the world, to feel the country was yours, to never question who you were. Under the porch light that was already flashing, he smiled his brilliant smile at her again, and they shook hands in the friendliest manner as they said good night.

That Friday evening, she watched television with two other girls in the dorm who did not have dates either. Saturday she was in the midst of washing her hair and polishing her nails when she was called to the telephone. She still did not know people well enough for anyone to call her, she thought. It was Mike. He was apologetic. He knew it was very late, but, perhaps, if she was free, would she like to go to a movie? Her pride debated with her inclination, and her pride lost. She accepted. He said he would pick her up at seven.

It was their first formal date, she told herself, and as such, special. She finished drying her hair and set it briefly on large rollers before going through her closet to decide on what to wear. She settled on a sleeveless linen shift, pale ivory like her skin and guaranteed to bring out the rich cocoa brown of her hair and eyes. She made up her face carefully, outlining her eyes with a soft brown pencil, but nothing like Consuelo would. The air force lieutenant she had dated in San Antonio had once remarked that he found the Catholic school girls' ladylike appearance "damned sexy." And as she finished dressing—crisp dress, pale stockings and beige pumps—and combed out her hair, shining and fresh-smelling, flipping up at the ends, almost touching her shoulders, she knew that the Sisters at Sacred Heart would find nothing to complain about in her appearance. They insisted on turning out ladies, as well as scholars, at Sacred Heart, but they also turned out sexy girls, as the lieutenant had said.

She was ready by six-thirty, and when he arrived at quarter to seven, she was already waiting for him in the parlor. They smiled shyly at each other, a little embarrassed at their own eagerness. But underneath his embarrassment she could also sense admiration.

"You look so nice," he finally said. "I thought we could walk to campus, go to the union movie, but if you'd rather not, I'll go get my car and we could go somewhere else. I'm not dressed for it, but I could go get a coat, and we could go dancing."

She was touched by his apology, but she didn't think he was inappropriately dressed—neat khaki trousers and freshly ironed madras shirt. She said he looked fine and going to the union movie was fine, too. And, since campus was only four blocks away, they would walk.

They were forty-five minutes early for the next feature, so they sat out on the student union patio, under large oak trees, and talked. She had come to love their talks, the probing of each other's personality, the gradual discovery of each other's lives and pasts, a little at a time, almost like a mental strip tease.

He told her about his grandparents, the Minnesota farmers who had come to South Texas with little money but much determination and had bought land to farm. At first they had relied on the unreliable rains, but soon they had put in irrigation wells, which allowed them to produce more and to buy more land. Then oil was discovered on the land in the 1940's, and by the end of the decade, the older Andersons had moved from their modest farmhouse to a fine house on Ocean Drive, overlooking the Bay of Corpus Christi. Mike's grandfather had been dead for ten years, and his oldest son, Mike's uncle Bob, now lived in the house with his family. His widowed grandmother also lived with them. Mike recalled the family barbecues on the lawn when the four Anderson children, Mike's uncle Bob, Mike's father, and two aunts and their children—twelve cousins in all—and their friends would gather for family holidays. On the Fourth of July and Labor Day, in particular, they would have barbecues. The children would play out on the lawn under the indulgent eyes of the grownups until the late afternoon became night, and then they played and laughed under the moonlight with the constant roar of the waves in the background.

Margo repressed a sigh as she listened to this description. She could see it all, just like a movie, a Hollywood movie with blond all-American actors, or maybe it was like *Giant*, with the Anglo-Saxon masters and the Mexican serfs.

He was talking now about picnics on the beach. Did she go to the beach often?

Should she tell him about the time her mother and grandmother had gone to Corpus Christi to see a doctor for her grandmother's arthritis? Her father did not like for his wife to drive those desolate country roads, so the two women had taken the bus to town. They had come back tight-lipped and pale, and Margo's mother had said, her voice shaking in hardly more than a whisper, that they had been forced to sit at the back of the bus, where the "coloreds" sat, as the driver said.

No, Margo felt the anecdote would not be conducive to a lighthearted exchange of reminiscences. It would probably embarrass him, and it certainly humiliated her.

Mike was already on to another question. "Margo," he was musing, "that's an unusual name. I've never known a girl named Margo before. Is it your real name or a nickname?"

It was the name she had chosen as preferable to "Margarita," which was as Mexican as the drink, but superior to "Margie," the name given to her by the teachers at the Los Encinos Sam Houston High School.

"It's short for Margot," she fibbed. "That was my grandmother's name—my father's mother, who was part French." Her grandmother had been another Margarita, and the story of the French soldier who had come with the Emperor Maximilian and who had stayed behind in Mexico and married an Ancira girl had never been confirmed.

Margo realized that in the game of mental strip tease they might play, she hid more than she revealed. But was he hiding anything? Did he have a girlfriend, for example, who had left him free for the summer? She did not ask any questions, though; she might not have liked the answers.

They sat through the movie, which was a comedy with a European location. Their shoulders brushed against each other until, in the time-honored fashion, he rested his arm on the back of the seat and then gradually let it slide down until it came to rest around her shoulders. Afterwards, they walked out of the theater hand in hand, and he suggested they stop at a coffee house recently opened. The place was lighted by dim red and blue bulbs, the light made more hazy by the thick smoke in the room. People sat on large cushions on the floor and listened to a Black blues singer while waitresses brought cups of espresso or cappuccino. She thought that he seemed out of place in these bohemian surroundings and wondered why he had brought her there.

They left the coffee house close to midnight and walked slowly back to her dorm, still hand in hand. He did not say good night upon arriving, however, but lingered on the veranda and gradually steered her to the short leg of the "L" of the porch, where the light was dim. He kissed her there and, without much prompting, she kissed him too. They began hesitantly, but soon their fervor increased. The intensity of her reaction surprised her. She suddenly realized how much she had been wanting him to kiss her. They remained pressed close against each other, their mouths searching eagerly for each other's lips, ears, throat, any non-forbidden part of the anatomy, until the porch lights flickered to signal curfew. Mike pulled himself away and said good night.

They fell into the habit of meeting every evening at the library and going for coffee afterwards. He would then walk her to the dorm where they would say good night on the dark end of the porch. She began to feel that they had always been together.

One evening, contrary to her custom, Consuelo was present at dinner. After the meal, she further surprised Margo by going upstairs with her and announcing that she was going to the library. As Margo was obviously preparing to do the same, she felt compelled to invite her roommate to join her. All the way to the library, while Consuelo chatted about people and places Margo did not know, Margo mentally kicked herself. She did not want Consuelo along when she was going to meet Mike. Consuelo was not a girl easily overlooked. Mike would probably fall for her. For once, the French Symbolists did not hold her attention as she read her assignment.

Shortly before ten, she saw Mike walk into the room; he knew where she usually sat and now scanned the room in her direction. When he caught her eye, he waved and gestured that he would be in the lobby. Margo gathered her books and, walking a fine line between inclination and courtesy, informed Consuelo that she was going to meet a friend.

"I think I'll go too," said Consuelo, stifling a yawn. Margo emerged from the reading room trailed by her roommate. There was nothing to be done but perform the introductions. Mike graciously included Consuelo in the invitation to go for coffee. Margo's heart sank further when Consuelo accepted.

They walked across the street to the coffee shop and, once inside, found their usual table. Mike went to the serving counter and got three coffees for them, and then and there began the usual preliminary conversation of what is your major and where are you from. Margo found, to her surprise—for she had yet to have a sustained conversation with her roommate—that Consuelo was majoring in anthropology, at least for the time being, and minoring in archeology. "Ruins fascinate me, you know. Especially in South America. Machu Picchu and the Incas. It's a good excuse to travel, anyway." Her father, she continued, was an engineer with an international construction company, and her family had lived in or visited most parts of the world. What other fascinating revelations Consuelo would have made were left in suspense when she spied three foreign students walking in the door and interrupted her conversation to wave at them.

"That's Ahmad," she said, "let me go say hello to him." After a few minutes of talking to the trio, she walked with them to a table.

Mike and Margo had fallen silent, watching the encounter, and now Mike finally said, "She seems to know them very well. Some girls really go for those desert jocks. Must be all the money they have." Margo was not sure whether to be glad that Consuelo was thus dismissed from his thoughts or to feel uneasy at his reason for doing so.

When it came time to leave, Margo caught Consuelo's attention and gestured, pointing to the door to convey their intention. Consuelo walked back to the table and picked up her books. "I'll catch up with you later at the dorm. I'm staying a little longer. We're having a fabulous conversation."

The following evening Consuelo reverted to her routine, and Margo went alone to the library to meet Mike. They studied together and, at nine-thirty, in unison, they put away their books and went for their usual nightcap. Later, as he walked her to the dorm, he asked her if she thought Consuelo would like to go out with his friend Jay. They could double date on Saturday evening. Margo had seen Jay only once, and briefly. She remembered him as tall and wiry, with dark hair and eyes and very black eyebrows. She thought him somewhat sardonic, but she could not be sure from the brief introduction. Margo agreed, somewhat tentatively, to broach the subject to Consuelo, which she did when Consuelo made her last minute arrival. To Margo's surprise, Consuelo agreed readily.

Saturday, at seven o'clock in the evening the sun still lingered, streaking the western sky with orange where it met the hills. The late June heat rose from the pavement as a reminder of the day it had been—and would be again on Sunday. By seven, Consuelo and Margo were ready. Consuelo wore a bold print of cobalt and green, a sleeveless shift that barely reached her knees, and Margo a pale yellow sundress. Both were festive but casual, since they did not know what the evening plans would be. "We'll probably go drink beer," Consuelo prophesized, "or buy a bottle and go somewhere for setups and dancing." She was right the first time.

Mike and Jay had decided to go to Scholz' beer garden, a traditional watering hole for politicians and students for almost a hundred years. Margo, who did not like beer, kept from saying so. She had heard so much about the place that she was glad to be finally going there, even if she had to nurse one beer all night long.

As they approached the beer garden, Mike, who was driving, turned to her and said. "I hope you girls have ID's. They're pretty sticky about them here."

Margo shook her head. "I'm not twenty-one yet."

"Well, neither am I," said Consuelo, "but that's no problem, I've got an ID."

Margo turned around to look at her roommate, and Consuelo hastened to explain: "My older sister and I look very much alike. She's out of the country, and she let me use her driver's license."

Jay, who had been silent after the introductions, put his arm around Consuelo's shoulders and gave her a quick squeeze, saying, "A girl after my own heart."

At Scholz's they sat in metal folding chairs around a picnic table under large pecan trees while waiters ran constantly from the bar, which was inside (and undoubtedly air conditioned, thought Margo longingly), carrying two or three heavy pitchers of beer at a time. They ordered a pitcher and three glasses and a Coke for Margo. All the tables seemed to be full. Conversation was difficult over the babble of voices, music amplified by loudspeakers concealed in the tree branches and the incongruous sound of falling bowling pins. Mike explained that there was a bowling alley next door.

During a lull in the music, while Consuelo remarked on the absurdity of not being able to get a mixed drink in Texas and of having to lug a bottle of bourbon in a brown paper bag when you went to a club, the talk turned to bars they had visited. Margo found herself the center of conversation when she mentioned the only bar she had ever been in, the Cadillac Bar in Nuevo Laredo. It was a hit; Mike had been there too. It was a real classic, he said. They had Pancho Villa's saddle there. Everybody should visit the Cadillac Bar, at least once. The drinks were great too. Yeah, Jay said, almost snickering, there was nothing like going to Mexico for a good time, why *don't* we go to Mexico? Margo was momentarily puzzled until she realized that when these people said Mexico, they did not mean Mexico City, as people back home did. They were talking about the border.

Soon Consuelo was asking, well, why don't we go to Mexico, and Mike said fine, but when, and then the logical answer presented itself: "Next weekend, of course. It's the Fourth of July."

"We would have to leave on Friday," Mike was already planning, "Friday afternoon at the latest. It's about a four-hour trip, to drive to Laredo, I mean. We don't want to spend the Fourth on the road."

Margo's thoughts were racing, could she go? Would her parents approve of the trip? No, of course not, they would never approve of an overnight trip, a weekend with three people they had never met, two of whom were of the opposite sex. She didn't have to tell her parents about it, but what if they found out? How? An accident on the road, or she might run into somebody they knew. . . .

"What about it, Margo, will you go?" Mike was asking.

"I don't know . . . I don't know if I can." Inspiration came suddenly. "I have a paper due on Monday after the Fourth."

"We'll be back on Sunday afternoon. And we'll make sure you start working on it tomorrow. C'mon, honey, say you'll go." He put his arm around her waist and gave her a gentle squeeze to punctuate his plea.

"I'd like to," she said softly, "let me see if I can."

"It's a date," Jay pronounced, pounding on the table. "We'll go to Mexico. We'll have a great time—get drunk, visit Boys' Town."

Margo started to shake her head and began to say she probably couldn't go, but Mike gave her another hug and told her not to mind Jay, he was just being an ass. Jay would behave himself, Mike would make sure of it.

On the way back to the dorm, Mike held her hand in between shifting gears. He smiled at her and whispered, "Say yes. I don't want to go without you," which made her knees go weak. Consuelo and Jay nuzzled in the back seat and generally acted as if they were very glad they had met. They kissed goodnight, briefly, because the curfew light was already flashing. Margo promised Mike she would let him know her decision about the trip by Wednesday, at the latest.

Margarita

On Tuesday evening he told her that he loved her while he kissed her. She was not even sure he had realized what he was saying, but that answered the question for her. The following evening, as soon as she saw him in the library, she told him she had decided to go to the border with them, after all. The next thing was to devise the strategy to keep her parents from accidentally finding out about the trip.

They left Friday at midafternoon because Margo had stubbornly refused to cut her one o'clock class. By three o'clock she and Consuelo were signed out for the weekend, giving the name of a friend of Consuelo's parents as their destination.

"She lives in San Antonio," Consuelo explained, "and I always go there on weekends. I mean, I always put down that there is where I am going."

They rode in Mike's car, a 1960 Chevrolet Impala, which had been his mother's until she had gotten a Cadillac for her birthday and given the Impala to him. The car windows were rolled down, by necessity, and the wind that rushed in burned their faces like the exhaust from a furnace. Mike told them his mother's new car had a wonderful air conditioner. His next car would be air conditioned, for sure. They were all in high spirits, though, joking and singing along with the Beatles on the car radio, even as they were driving into the sun.

After they came out of San Antonio, they left behind the rolling pasture land and the hills that had followed them in the distance. Oaks and elms now gave way to stunted mesquites and an occasional huisache. This was the beginning of the brush country, thick, thorny scrub brush, as impenetrable as a forest in parts. Where the brush had been cleared by some enterprising rancher, though, the grass was singed brown. They passed small towns, some of only a few hundred people and with one paved street—the one they were on. They all reminded Margo of Los Encinos. At one of them, midway between Austin and Laredo, they stopped for gasoline and Cokes. As they stood out on the pavement, while the attendant filled up the car, Jay began to complain. What a Godforsaken place, how could people live here, nothing but heat and dust, not even a single shade tree. He knew it was hot all over Texas, but this must be the deepest pit in hell.

"Now you know why the Spaniards called this country the *brasada*," said Margo, surprising herself for remembering this little-known fact of Texas history. She did not know where she had heard it, probably from her grandmother.

"What's that? You know I don't speak the lingo," Jay responded suspiciously.

"It means a bed of coals."

"You can say that again. We should have let Mexico have it. You might as well be in Mexico, anyway, the way they chatter down here." This was directed at the two service station attendants who carried on their conversation in Spanish, oblivious to their audience. Margo was glad when Mike got his change, and they got back in the car. She had not wanted another lecture about "this is America, why don't they speak American." Consuelo, Margo noted, had yet to complain about the heat or the scenery; this perhaps portended well for her future as an anthropologist or archeologist.

It was not yet eight o'clock and even hotter still when they reached Laredo. They debated whether to eat first or find a motel with reasonably priced rooms. They drove up and down the main street, passing some ten or twelve motels before stopping at one that looked clean but modest. They were not in luck; it was full. They began again, and with the same results. By the fourth or fifth try they began to get anxious.

"It's the Fourth of July weekend, and we're full of tourists. They're having bullfights across the river on Sunday," one reception clerk finally explained. Margo told herself she should have thought of that. Jay was definitely on edge now, and even Consuelo began to fret, complaining that she was dying for a shower.

They must have tried all ten or twelve motels without any luck. However, at one of them, among the least prepossessing, the clerk said he was holding two rooms, but the people had not arrived yet. If they were not checked in by nine, he would let them have the rooms. Mike suggested they go get something to eat in the meantime; they would be back before nine, he assured the clerk. They had hamburgers and Cokes at a restaurant some two blocks away from the motel they had dubbed "The Last Chance." The restaurant was air conditioned, and the cool air revived them briefly. At ten to nine, while they were still eating, Mike said he would just drive back to the motel to be sure he was there at nine so the clerk wouldn't give the rooms to somebody else.

He left, and Jay and Consuelo soon fell into a rather querulous conversation while Margo relived her main concern of "what if my parents found out." Mike returned some thirty minutes later to a cold, half-eaten hamburger, but he had two room keys. They paid for the food and got back in the car for the two block drive. After Mike parked the car, and they were unloading their bags, Consuelo turned to Margo and said, "I'll toss you to see who gets the shower first. After that it's sleep for me." Margo smiled at her, genuinely liking her for the first time and mentally thanking her for so swiftly answering the awkward questions that hung unasked of who would sleep with whom.

"Yes," she agreed, "I'm falling asleep on my feet," and they left the men to go find their own room.

The next morning they went back to the same restaurant, and while they ate breakfast they discussed the itinerary for the day. They were going across the river, to Mexico, as Jay said, there was no question of that, but what to do first once there. They decided to let Margo be their guide, and her suggestion was that they should park the car close to the International Bridge, on the U.S. side, and then walk across the bridge. They would avoid the heavy Saturday traffic that way.

They left the car by the old plaza around which the city had been founded in the mid-eighteenth century and set out walking. A soft breeze was blowing, alleviating the heat of the sun that was already beating down on them, and the walk was not unpleasant. The bridge was crowded with pedestrians and cars going in both directions. Consuelo and Jay stopped, along with other tourists, midway across the bridge to look down at the Rio Grande, flowing sluggishly below, but Margo averted her eyes. Heights gave her a queasy feeling. Jay was disappointed; the river was not very big, contrary to its name. Margo explained that there was a large dam upstream that controlled the flow.

At last they were across, barely nodding at the customs guard in passing, and the sounds and smells that Margo always associated with Mexican towns surrounded them. The smells were a mixture, she thought, of diesel fumes and the fruits from the street vendors' carts. The sounds were a confused din of shouts from the newspaper boys and lottery ticket vendors, car horns and the music blaring from record shops. She suggested that they walk up and down the main street first, just looking and window shopping. The sidewalks were crowded with tourists and vendors offering them everything from cheap leather wallets to paintings of bullfighters done on velvet. Margo told them they should wait before buying anything until they had looked in the shops.

By lunch time, they must have visited every shop on a five or six block stretch, Margo thought. They went to the Cadillac Bar, which Jay had wanted to visit from the moment they had set foot in Nuevo Laredo. It was full of tourists, and they had a long wait before they were served, but the food was good. They had seafood and roast cabrito, and Margo introduced them to the Ramos Gin Fizz, which tasted like a milk shake with a kick. They duly admired the saddle that was prominently displayed and that was reputed to have belonged to Pancho Villa. They read about the origins of the Cadillac Bar in New Orleans and about how, with the advent of Prohibition, it had relocated in Nuevo Laredo.

It was after two o'clock when they emerged from the cool dimness of the bar, and the sun beat down on them as if it had a personal grudge against them. They agreed that they would probably get sunstroke if they tried walking back to the car then, so they ambled down the main street again, staying under the awnings of the shops for shade as much as possible until they came to a plaza. It was relatively empty at that hour, only mad dogs and Americans being out in the sun then, and they sat on a marble bench under the largest tree. They carried on a fitful, disjointed conversation, punctuated by fanning themselves with a magazine they had found lying on the bench. Consuelo pointed out a café on the other side of the plaza, and they decided to stop suffering and go in there and drink something. Mike said he was thirsty, but didn't want to drink the water, so Consuelo told him to drink beer, this was some of the best beer in the world.

They sat there some two hours, drinking beer. Margo drank lemonade, to Mike's consternation; he kept saying the water in it would probably make her sick. She assured him she always drank lemonade "if the place looked clean." Jay had discovered the merits of Mexican beer, and they eventually left the café to get him to stop drinking it. He weaved slightly as he walked, and Margo began to worry about making it back to the car. They finally hit upon the idea of riding back to the bridge in one of the horse-drawn buggies that carried tourists around downtown. Jay's spirits soared, and he enjoyed himself immensely, waving at pedestrians and cars and insisting loudly that he wanted to visit Boys' Town and see the whores. Margo, afraid that the driver would take him seriously, hastened to assure the man that they wanted to go to the bridge. She began to wish they had never made the trip, and only prayed they would get across the bridge and through customs safely and without further embarrassment. As they walked across the bridge, though, Jay seemed relatively subdued, merely trying on the same stale joke on the customs guard: when asked if they were bringing back any liquor, he replied, patting his stomach and grinning, "Only inside." The guard had heard it before; he waved them on without a smile.

As they drove back to the motel, Jay asked if there would be any fireworks that evening.

"I don't think so," said Margo. "I've never heard of them

having fireworks on the Fourth of July. New Year's Eve, yes."

"We might as well be in a foreign country. It's un-American to have bullfights for the Fourth of July but no fireworks," Jay continued to grumble.

"It's probably too hot for fireworks," Consuelo said calmly. "Anyway, the bullfights are tomorrow—and they *are* in another country. Mexico is across the river."

"You couldn't tell it. It all looks the same on both sides of the river."

"Why don't we go swimming when we get back to the motel?" Consuelo had stepped into the role of peacemaker, thought Margo, and she was glad of it.

As soon as they were back at the motel, Consuelo and Jay got into their swimsuits and jumped in the pool, calling to Margo and Mike to join them. Margo shook her head; she had not even brought a swimsuit. Instead, she went to her room and stepped into the shower. Her head was beginning to ache from the heat, but the water trickling down her face and the back of her neck was soothing. She felt much better by the time she had dried off and put on fresh clothes.

Margo went outside and watched the two in the pool until Mike joined her, soon afterwards. He had obviously showered and changed and had that air of crispness that seldom left him. Margo looked up affectionately at him. He motioned her to sit next to him on a glider under the scanty shade of a palm tree. They sat in silence, his arm draped around the back of the glider, his fingertips lightly touching her bare shoulder, until the other two, laughing and breathless, came out of the water and dried themselves. The sun was going down, and the heat now was more like the afterglow of embers rather than the fire raining down from above it was earlier. Jay and Consuelo spread out their towels on a small patch of grass at Mike and Margo's feet and lay on their backs. Margo caught fragments of their conversation, disjointed words only, and thought she must be dozing off.

Consuelo finally sat up and announced she was going back to her room to get out of her wet suit. Jay reached up and pulled her down again, and there followed a playful struggle that threatened to leave Consuelo with only a fragment of her swimsuit on. She finally got up and, rather crossly, told Jay to keep his paws off her and walked away. He scrambled up and ran after her. Soon they were out of sight as they rounded the corner that hid their rooms from view of the pool.

A family with three children then came out and took over the pool. In spite of their shouts, Margo felt herself lulled by the gentle rocking motion of the glider as Mike pushed it back with his foot. A feeling of contentment spread over her as they sat there, their bodies only brushing against each other.

She was glad the day was over; she doubted that she was particularly suited to be a tourist guide. Jay had been difficult, but, still, she was glad to be there with Mike in what was more her natural environment than Austin. It was good to hear Spanish again and to speak it. She remembered the first time she was away from home without her family. It was a school trip for a convention in West Texas. Three days of hearing and speaking only English. She told her best friend afterwards that her face muscles had begun to ache with the strain of smiling all the time and speaking nothing but English. At school they were forbidden to speak Spanish, received demerits (even whippings in grade school) if they were caught doing so, but after school Spanish was all they spoke. It was only when she went away to college that she realized that she spoke "with an accent," as someone put it. She immediately started working on shedding the telltale "Spanish accent," asking her speech teacher for help, imposing on herself the discipline of speaking only English, even with Teresita. Her face muscles became used to it.

It occurred to her that Consuelo and Jay had been gone much longer than necessary to change out of their wet swimsuits, and she wondered if they were in one of the rooms together. A mixture of excitement and unease went through her, and she thought, "I wish I knew how to handle this like Consuelo," and then, "I'm happy just as we are now," for Mike was speaking softly and had his arm around her.

She did not pay close attention to everything he said; it was enough that she could hear his voice and feel him next to her. He was talking about being out in the open sea in the Gulf, fishing; about his uncle Bob's boat, the Yacht Club, sailing in the bay. She wondered what her father would think of this Mike; this Mike was not an itinerant. Her mother would be pleased that he was going to study to be a doctor. Should she ask him home for Thanksgiving? She would be home for Labor Day. Would he be sailing out in the bay then? Perhaps he could come home to see her during the Labor Day weekend. He was telling her now about his mother, how crazy she was about taking photographs, especially at family gatherings. Last year on the Fourth of July they had had a cookout in the backyard, by the pool. She was taking pictures and wanted the perfect pose—he and his sisters and his father, all together. His mother kept walking backwards and looking through the lens until she fell, backwards, in the water, the deep end. The water was above her head, but she held up the camera as high as she could, kept it dry. They helped her out, laughing at her all the time. She was furious with them for laughing at her, but finally she ended up laughing, too, really good a sport. Margo smiled, too, at the image she conjured of his mother, wet and angry but blond and beautiful, like her son.

"She sounds like a lot of fun," she heard herself saying, drawling out the words lazily. "I can't wait to meet her."

"Oh, but I couldn't take you home. . . ." His words hung in the air for several seconds before she felt their impact like a solid blow. She went very still then, and felt as if she were shrinking in size by the minute. It was just like the time when she had first met him. The harsh words had come out of him without apology, and then the delayed contriteness followed. She felt the muscles in his arms contract now with tension, and then he said, sounding more regretful than contrite, though, "Oh, God, I am sorry. I didn't mean it like that . . ."

But how did he mean it, she asked herself as she got up, slowly and stiffly, like an old woman. "I am going back to my room. The heat is giving me a headache," she said in a tight, flat voice, unlike her own. He made as if to stop her, but then he let his arm fall, and she walked away, holding herself very straight.

As she approached her room, the thought struck her that Jay and Consuelo might be in there. "I'll kick them out, if I have to," she thought, savagely, for she had begun to feel her face burning red, and anger shook her body. The room was empty, though, cool and dark. The two must be next door in the dim, cool room, on fresh-smelling sheets . . . She closed the door behind her and shot the deadbolt.

She walked into the bathroom and turned on the light, peering at herself in the mirror above the sink. The color was draining from her face, leaving only a red flush on her throat. She slammed her hand against the edge of the sink. "You stupid fool, you damned, stupid fool. And to think I was falling for him," she whispered, still looking at herself in the mirror. "And to think I would have probably gone to bed with him," was her next thought. She felt a cold sweat break out all over her body, and nausea gripped her for a minute. "Oh, God, it was that damned seafood," she said and, turning on the cold tap, stuck her head under the water. She felt better after a minute or so. Finally, she straightened up and, taking a towel, rubbed her face and her hair dry.

"And now what are you going to do? What am I to do? Those two will eventually emerge from the passion pit next door, and what will I do then? I just couldn't bear to face them. I must think of a way to get away, get back to Austin without them." In moments of crisis, Margo resorted to these conversations with herself. "But how, where can I go?" She could not see herself walking, overnight bag in hand, to another hotel. She had enough money to ride the bus back to Austin tomorrow, but what to do tonight? She was staring at the telephone when inspiration struck. Teresita, of course.

She dialed Teresita's number and knocked on the table, hoping it was wood and not plastic. A young voice answered in Spanish. Yes, Teresita was home, wait a minute, said Teresita's sister. Margo was so relieved, she sat down weakly on the bed. A minute went by while she gripped the receiver anxiously, and then there was Teresita, exclaiming with delight, what a wonderful surprise, haven't seen you since last Christmas, where are you, you've got to come over. Margo explained. She had come down for the weekend with these other three people from Austin, a boy and a couple who wanted to see the border, but—here she hesitated—she didn't like the way they were acting. Ah, Teresita understood, give them an inch and they take a yard. Why didn't Margo come and stay with her; she would come and pick her up, where was she? Margo told her.

Hastily, Margo stuffed her belongings into the overnight bag and then, unable to shake off ingrained courtesy, wrote a short note to Consuelo, explaining that she was going to visit an old roommate and would return to Austin on her own. She propped up the note against Consuelo's makeup case, certain that it would be found there. Some twenty minutes later Teresita was knocking at the door. Margo opened it cautiously, then, seeing who it was, grabbed her bag and quietly closed the door behind her. Anyone seeing her would assume she was sneaking out without paying the bill, which in a way she was, she thought.

Teresita wanted to talk before they went home, since her brothers and their girlfriends were there, and it was a madhouse. They went to a drive-in restaurant and asked for curb service. They both ordered Cokes, and Margo, suddenly realizing she had not had supper, also ordered a cheese sandwich. "So, now tell me about Europe. What about tonight, though, did you end up with some creep; was he lecherous?" Mike's face, his voice, his scent were suddenly before Margo once more, and something wrenched inside her, but then she felt her cheeks burning again, as if he had left the imprint of a slap on her face. She told Teresita that she had described the situation just right, and then went on to tell her about the spring semester in Europe.

As they drove home through the dark streets, Margo tasted humiliation, bitter as gall, rising again in her throat, in a surge of self-loathing. The next moment, though, she thought, "I can't go on like this for the rest of my life. I am who I am. If others don't like me, it's their problem. I belong in this country as much as they do, down here even more than they because we were here first."

She wondered what explanation Mike would eventually give to Jay for her sudden departure. The García blood reasserted itself in her then, shoving aside good manners, and she thought, "I don't care what they think about my leaving tonight. If they don't like it, screw them." She repressed an impulse to giggle. "Or better still: don't screw them."

They left the car in the driveway and went into the house, where all the lights were blazing. Teresita's younger sister and older brother were sprawled out on the living room floor, playing Monopoly, while her parents sat around the dining table, conversing with their son's fiancée. There were handshakes and hugs as Margo greeted each one, until Teresita broke in and said that she wanted to show Margo to the guest bedroom.

Margo followed her friend up the stairs, but before they reached the room, she asked, "Do you mind if I call my parents? I'll make it collect."

As Margo heard the telephone ringing, one hundred miles away, she felt a great desire to cry. "Not now," she told herself, and then she heard the soft sound of her father's voice saying, "Hello" in an accent that was noticeable even in his surroundings.

"Papá," she said, "this is Margarita."

The Kid
from the Alamo

When I saw him again, thirty years later, he did not look like anybody's idea of a hero. It was a Friday afternoon, and I was going home because my brother Rufus' youngest boy was getting married the following day. I was by myself, since my wife had to work that Saturday. She's a nurse, and that weekend she was on duty at the hospital. Our two kids, Ricky, who is ten, and Laura, who is eight, were staying with their grandmother, my mother-in-law, till Sunday.

It was in late September, still hot, as it always is all through September, when I headed south. I had just passed the city limits when I saw, looming up to my right, an enormous sign with "Gas" and "Eats." I didn't remember seeing it the last time I passed this way, but that was several months before, so maybe I had just forgotten. I decided I might as well top off the gas tank and pick up a couple of six packs so I wouldn't be arriving empty handed.

I pulled in, used the self-serve pump, and then went inside to pay and get the beer. After the glare of the sun, it took me a minute or so to get my eyes used to the dim light inside. I took off my dark glasses, but even so, it was still dark—just one fluorescent light above and no windows, except the front one.

I looked around. It was a large room; at one end there were some five or six tables with chairs around them, all empty now. The far wall was all taken up by glass-fronted coolers. I made my way there and picked up a six-pack of lite beer for me and one of regular for Rufus. On my way in I had half noticed the man standing behind the counter, just inside the door, as it opened to the left. I looked at him then as I gave him my credit card and a twenty-dollar bill for the beer. While he printed the receipt and gave me the change I kept looking at him, now that my eyes were better accustomed to the light.

There was nothing unusual about the man; he was just somebody maybe a little older than me. He was shorter than me and thinner, but he had wiry muscles, and you could tell he was strong. His hair was combed straight back in a way that looked sort of old fashioned. He wore a white, long-sleeved shirt with the cuffs rolled back, and I could see part of a small tattoo on his left hand, above a gold ring shaped like a horseshoe and studded with little diamonds. He handed me the receipt, I signed it and gave him back his copy, my eyes going no higher than his chest. The top two buttons of his shirt were undone, showing a gold St. Christopher medal on a chain around his neck.

He noticed that I was staring at him and looked at me as if to say, "Anything else I can do for you, buddy." I said, "thank you" right away so he wouldn't think I was being rude. I was just thinking what an odd, blank expression his eyes had, when I realized that I had better not look at him too much or he might get mad. I looked past him to the sign on the wall above him instead. It said, "O. Esparza, Prop."

All of a sudden I saw long-sleeved shirts buttoned to the top and baggy khaki pants bending at the instep, dragging in the dust of a school playground. Before I knew it I was asking, "Osvaldo?"

You could tell that he was immediately wary, not of anything in particular, but just as if that was how he often was.

"Oswald Esparza is my name, yes. What can I do for you?"

That didn't sound like he wanted a conversation, but I went on. I asked him, "Didn't you go to school in Poggendorf? Junior high, wasn't it?"

He just looked at me, not saying anything, but, like an idiot, I kept on talking. "You know, Poggendorf, just down the road, forty-five miles down the road from here, going south. I remember now, it wasn't junior high. It was elementary school. Sixth grade. Miss Gibbs, don't you remember?"

For some reason it seemed very important to me that he should remember, and, racking my brains for something to jog his memory, I finally said the obvious. "I am Rubén Morales. I was in school with you."

Recognition flickered for a moment in his eyes; then they went blank again. "Ah, yes," he said in an unusually low voice. I wondered if there was something wrong with his throat. "I had forgotten," he continued. "That was so long ago. I only lived there for a little while. I don't go down that way anymore."

I wanted to stick out my hand and call him *Vato* and start talking in Spanish, throwing in a few *pachuco* words that I had learned on the playground from him, but he was standing behind the counter with the look of "What else can I do for you, and will that be all?" I got stubborn. I thought that meeting him again after all these years was important. Why didn't he? I wanted him to say something, so I ignored the hint and started talking about myself, hoping that he would reciprocate and tell me what he was doing here and what he had done before.

I told him that I was living in San Antonio and that I was going to Poggendorf for my nephew's wedding. I told him that I was working for the federal government and that I was married and had two kids. I told him about how when I had finished high school, I had enlisted in the Air Force and how, when my term was up, I had re-enlisted, which maybe had not been too smart since it was in the middle of the Vietnam War, but I had really spent all my time in Europe. I had been lucky, I guess. When I got out of the service I had come home and used my veteran's benefits and gone to college. I had gotten a degree in business and gone back to work for the government.

He stood there, listening patiently and politely but without much interest. I asked him if he had been in San Antonio all this time, without knowing exactly what I meant by "all this time." I didn't think that he had been in this café since the end of the sixth grade. How long had he had this business, I asked.

He had opened it about six months ago, he told me. I looked around and noticed that the Formica-topped tables still had a shiny look to them. He had been in California some years, had owned a couple of trucks there, but had gotten sick for a while and decided to leave the road. I asked him about his parents. His father had died several years back; his mother lived in San Antonio.

While I was remembering that his father had been a truck driver and that his mother had run the bar in Poggendorf where truck drivers would stop for hamburgers and beer, and thinking how he had taken after both of them, a truck pulled up outside. Two men came in, and Osvaldo—or Oswald, as he called himself now—explained to them that the kitchen wasn't open yet, but that he had cold sandwiches. He went with them to the coolers and got them each a sandwich, a beer for one and a Coke for the other. I lost him after that.

He stood by their table, talking to the driver and his friend about how the onion crop had been this year in the Valley and how the citrus was likely to turn out. I stood by the cash register, but I guess I did not really expect him to pick up the thread of his life history again. So, after I paid for a stick of chewing gum (as an excuse to get him back to the counter), we just said a few more words, and I left.

I got back on the road and soon left behind the last of the city traffic. It was not five yet, so I didn't have to contend with the commuters, and I almost had the road to myself. South of San Antonio, the oaks start to thin out, and you begin to see more mesquite and huisache; it's the beginning of the brush country. Along the road to Poggendorf, though, there are still a few enormous oaks standing alone in the middle of cleared fields, and tall pecans line the creek beds. I have always thought that this particular stretch of road is very pretty.

A little to the west of the road to Poggendorf the site of an old battle between the Spanish royalists and the Mexican insurgents is supposedly located. It happened around the time of the Mexican War of Independence of 1810, when this was all part of Mexico. The battle is said to have been the bloodiest ever fought in Texas, and just recently some historians have started writing about it. Some people even had a re-enactment of the battle in August. It's mainly Anglos from out of state who are interested in that kind of stuff, though. The locals never bother about it. I certainly never read about this Battle of Medina in any school books.

Which reminded me of Osvaldo and the history class in the sixth grade.

I don't remember Osvaldo before the sixth grade, so I am pretty sure that he was in school with us only for that year. We didn't know much about him, but what everybody in the school did know was that Osvaldo was a *pachuco*. We had never had a *pachuco* in school before, and probably had not seen very many of them in real life, but we knew what they looked like. They looked like Osvaldo: long, baggy, khaki pants and long-sleeved shirts buttoned all the way up. They also wore their hair combed in a pompadour up front and with a ducktail in back, sort of like early Elvis Presley.

This was 1958 or 1959, and the heyday of *pachucos* was already over. Some people said that *pachucos* went back to the early forties and remembered the Zoot Suit Riots in California which had happened at that time. They had been strongest in the barrios in California and in the larger cities of the Southwest, like Albuquerque and San Antonio. Also, it was funny, but *pachucos* had been mostly Mexican-American and not Mexican-Mexican. Anyway, *pachucos* were when I was a kid what the hippies were later: something that your parents hoped you would not grow up to be.

We knew that Osvaldo was a *pachuco* because he dressed like one and because he slouched when he walked and snapped his fingers when he talked. Our parents—mine and my friends'—wanted us to stay away from Osvaldo. Respectable Mexican-American families were always worried that the Anglos, as usual, would not make distinctions and lump all Mexicans as *pachucos*. To us kids, he was someone like a pirate out of a story or an outlaw from the Wild West. There was an air of danger about him, and we didn't know whether to imitate him or be afraid of him.

My friends and I did not know if Osvaldo was a *pachuco* because of his unusual family situation or if the whole family just lived by an entirely different set of rules from the rest of us. In a small town where everybody knew everybody else, down to their grandparents, very little was known about Osvaldo's family or his home life. Most grown-ups thought there was something wrong with the family where the father was gone most of the time, driving trucks all over the country, although they knew that he hauled produce, including some local crops.

The truck driving might have passed if he had been from the area, but nobody knew where Mr. Esparza came from. One day he had just shown up with his wife and son in a place like Poggendorf where nobody moved in unless they had a very good reason to do so. He was gone, often for weeks at a time, and then, to top everything off, his wife began running a beer joint just off the highway. It had belonged to Manuel Rosales, but he had gotten too old and sick to run it anymore and had been on the verge of closing it down, when Mrs. Esparza leased it from him.

Sixth-grade kids are regular beasts. The boys, anyway. I remember that we alternated between throwing mud balls at the girls and chasing them around the playground to grab and grope—a couple of them, in particular, who were beginning to show breasts. But not Osvaldo. Without having to run after any of the girls, he smuggled a couple of them into his house when his parents were gone and groped at leisure.

There was another thing that impressed us about Osvaldo. His parents seemed to leave him alone. His mother didn't nag; his father didn't threaten to break his head open if he did or didn't do this or that. It was such a contrast to my situation. Not that my mother nagged. She simply sat in silence while my father turned beet red shouting at me, wondering how he could have had such a dumb kid (if I got bad grades), or such a clumsy kid (if I got hurt playing baseball), until she would say, "Calm yourself, Rufino. Remember your blood pressure," which was like turning up the fire under boiling water.

I had come to the conclusion that it was not a question of whether my parents loved me. It was just that I had been born at the wrong time. I had been born too late, when my parents were already beginning to have grandchildren. I was the youngest of six, four boys and two girls, and there was an eight-year difference between my brother Roberto, the closest one to me, and myself. My father had forgotten by then what it was like to deal with an eleven-year-old.

My brother, Rufino, Jr., was the oldest. He was thirty at the time and had just gotten married and moved to a house in town with his wife, Nilda, and was still working in the peanut warehouse, where he had been since he got out of high school, except for his stint in the Army. My two sisters came next. They were Yolanda and Helen. (She had been baptized María Elena, but after she got married and moved to San Antonio, she became Helen.) They had both gotten married right after high school and now had two kids each. Then came my brothers, Roel and Roberto. Since my mother's name was Rosa and my father was Rufino, my mother had decided that all the kids' names would begin with "R." She had stuck with the plan with the boys, but somehow she forgot with the girls.

When I was in the sixth grade, I had been the only kid at home for over a year, and I couldn't remember if my father's temper had always been that short, or if I was the only one who made him mad. Everybody said my father's temper was like a match—it didn't take much to set it off. Looking back, I think his bad humor might have been caused by the fact that he didn't know what to do with so many kids. He had been an only child himself, and his own father had known that what he had would all go to his son. But with six children, how was my father to provide for all of us?

My father belonged to the generation and the kind of

people that believed that you had to leave something to your children. You had to keep what you had inherited, and you had to add to that what you had made, yourself. His father, my grandfather, had come to South Texas around 1918 with a wife and a child, my father. The old man was a colonel in the Mexican Revolution. He was with Carranza's army, I think. Anyway, he was with somebody who was on the losing side towards the end of the Revolution, because he had to get out of the country. The old man did not come out completely on the losing side, though, since he came out with some money. With that money, he began to buy small parcels of land south of San Antonio, mainly from other Mexicans, the few that had not yet been squeezed out by the Anglos. On some three hundred acres or so, he ran some cattle and made a living for his family. That was the land that my father inherited.

My father continued his father's practice of buying any surrounding tracts that came available, until he ended up with a little over six hundred acres. He struck it really lucky in the early forties when an oil company drilled two wells on the property. The production ended after a few years, but my father took the money from the royalties and drilled water wells with it, so that when the oil people left, we had water for irrigating crops. That's how he got into farming. He still kept some cattle, but, after some time, most of his income came from cotton and peanuts.

He was so proud of what he had managed to hold and acquire that it caused him grief at the thought of having it broken up after his death. One hundred acres for each of us wasn't going to keep anybody in business, and he knew how hard it was for brothers and sisters to run a ranch together. Finally, when I was about fifteen, he got us all together and told us what he had decided to do. Rufino, Jr., would get the land and the ranch house and live on the place. The rest of us would get in cash the equivalent of the land that would have come to us if he had divided the place equally.

I don't think that any of us really minded his decision. My sisters were living in town, where their husbands worked—

Yolanda in Poggendorf and Helen in San Antonio. Roel and Roberto were both in the service then and overseas, and we did not know if they planned to come back to live in Poggendorf because they were career Army. I was eager to get away and see the world, so the thought of having money instead of land was more agreeable.

I was in the Air Force when my father died, but I got leave to come home for the funeral. The old man had had a stroke several months before and had been pretty much incapacitated since then. In a way I was glad at his going, because I knew how much it hurt him to be an invalid. We were all at the funeral, except Roel, who was in a hospital in Japan, recuperating from a shattered leg he had gotten in Vietnam. He was lame after he recovered and eventually got a disability pension from the Army and came back to Poggendorf, where he is still working in the warehouse. After my father's death Rufus moved to the ranch with his family, where they still are. My mother lived with Rufus at the ranch for the next ten years or so until she died.

We got the cash that my father had promised us in place of the land. I saved my share and later used it to buy the house I live in now. Lord knows how hard it must have been for the old man to have put together that money, and, as a matter of fact, tightfisted as he was, he still couldn't save enough. Rufus had to sell his house in town after he moved back to the ranch, and he made up the difference to give the rest of us our share. He had promised the old man that he would do so.

I could see the water tower as I approached Poggendorf—not exactly a sprawling metropolis at population 1,500. I remember when it had been only 1,200. Poggendorf is a funny name for a town in South Texas, where most of the people are Mexican. Some of the old timers still call the place Los Robles, which was supposedly the name of a big ranch in the area until a German named Poggen had wandered in some one hundred years ago and taken it over. He had brought the railroad as well, creating Poggendorf in the process.

I bumped over the railroad tracks, past the peanut warehouse and mill, and spotted the Dairy Queen a block away. All of a sudden I wanted to stop for a while and get my thoughts in order before I saw the family. I also wanted a milkshake. I pulled into the parking lot and went in and ordered a grilled cheese sandwich and a chocolate milk shake.

I took a booth by a window. From where I sat I could see, past the Texaco service station on the corner, part of the elementary school. It was a new school, not the one I had gone to. This one had been built some fifteen years ago. My school, the old Elmer Poggen Elementary School, had been at the end of town, at the edge of the plowed fields so that farm kids, like myself, could reach it easily. Probably about half of the students had been from town, but the parents of the other half, the farmers and ranchers, paid most of the property taxes that supported the schools, so the school administrators accommodated them.

My father was one of a very small number of Mexicans in the county that owned land of any size. The population of the area was probably around seventy percent Mexican, but the land (for the most part) and the major businesses in town, like the warehouse and the mill, the Ford truck dealership and the auction house, were all owned by Anglos. My father used to say that he felt like a tight rope walker, keeping from caving in to the Anglos (he called them Gringos) while staying close enough to them to find out if they were going to try to put anything over on him.

The tight rope act may have caused enough stress to bring on the stroke, but it paid off with his kids. Poggendorf wasn't big enough to have segregated schools, like other towns did—for Mexicans and Anglos, that is, because I had never seen a black person south of San Antonio. In the forties, when Rufus had started school, all kids supposedly went to the same elementary school, but my father had found out, the first day of school, that the Mexican children were all put together in a couple of rooms by themselves. My father, himself, had been educated at home, on the ranch, by a schoolmaster paid by his father to teach him and other Mexican children from the nearby ranches. He had not been a student for very long, but had had a solid foundation in arithmetic and in reading and writing Spanish. He had also received English lessons from a retired schoolteacher in town. The school system, then, had been a surprise to him when he took Rufus that first day.

The school principal had explained that the Mexican children were kept apart because they did not speak English and often had problems that kept them from learning at the same pace as the Anglo children. My father had asked if, after the Mexican children had learned English and caught up in other ways, they were transferred to classes with the Anglos. The principal had been vague about what happened afterwards to the Mexican children, but my father noticed that there were very few of them beyond ten years or so.

The principal added that most of the children of Mexican parents were pulled out of school very early to help in the fields. My father responded that his kids would help in the fields in the summer when they were on vacation. In the meantime, he wanted his child to start school with the Anglos or wherever the kids that were not considered backward were.

He got his way, and all of us went to school in the regular classes, although by the time I came along things were not so bad. Elementary school was just one battle, though. My father had to fight another one when Rufus got to high school. Mexican kids were not expected to go to high school, but, again, Rufus was the trailblazer. Even my sisters finished high school. Some people told my father there was no sense in the girls getting a high school diploma since they were going to get married and stay home. The old man replied that there was no guarantee that his daughters would get married—or stay married—and that they might need to earn a living if they were single or widowed. Besides, he would add, Mexicans had enough disadvantages in this country without being ignorant, as well.

That was why my part in the school revolt hurt him so much.

This is where Osvaldo comes in. Osvaldo and Miss Gibbs and the Texas history class.

I remember the spring of the sixth grade. We were all feeling pretty frisky because in May we would be graduating from elementary school and going on to junior high in September. In junior high we would be doing important things, like playing football. In the meantime, we put up with the usual stuff, like English and arithmetic, geography and Texas history. Texas history was something that I wasn't particularly interested in. A few things about it struck me as odd, though. I remember that the textbook started at first with a few pages on the Indians, then there was a little about the Spanish explorers and how they called the place "Tejas," after an Indian tribe, and that the word meant "friends." Then there was another bit about the missionaries and the missions they built, several of which were just a ways up the road from us. Then it jumped to the arrival of the Anglos.

That is what struck me as odd. I mean, all you had to do was look around, and you would see that there were a lot of us, Mexicans, in Texas. So where did we come in? We came in at the Alamo, where we killed Davy Crockett, and at San Jacinto, where we were whipped by Sam Houston. That was it. Santa Anna and the wicked Mexicans were taken care of in a couple of chapters, and then we went on to the Civil War and a lot of boring governors after that. And not another Spanish name was mentioned again. Well, as I said, parts of Texas history bothered me, but I had more important things to think about, like baseball and keeping my father from chewing me out because I played too much and didn't study enough.

Then Miss Gibbs told us of her plan. She announced one day that she was aware that some of us might think that we had been going too quickly over our history book. I didn't think so, and I said so in a whisper to Pete Martínez, who sat in front of me. The reason for the fast pace, continued Miss Gibbs, was that she wanted us to finish the book early so that, starting next week, the first week in May, we could devote ourselves to studying in depth the most important part of the course: the Texas Revolution. We had already gotten an overview of the history of Texas; now we would study in detail its most glorious episodes. In this manner we would be able to appreciate fully the experiences that we would have during our class trip.

We all perked up at that. A class trip! Pete turned to look at me and gave me a thumbs-up sign. We were already thinking of all the things we could do without even knowing yet where we were going. Miss Gibbs proceeded to tell us that Mr. Ewing, the principal, had agreed for the school to sponsor a class trip for the graduating sixth graders. We would go for a day to San Antonio and spend several hours in the cradle of Texas liberty: the Alamo.

I had never been to the Alamo, and I didn't mind going, but there were other places that I would have rather gone to if I was going to spend the day in San Antonio. Everybody said how much fun it was to go through the Lone Star brewery, for example, but I didn't see the school sponsoring a class trip there, as I told Pete.

So we started reading again about Stephen F. Austin and the arrival of the Anglos in Texas with the permission of the Mexican government. We got as far as the Mexican government reneging on some deal it had made with the Anglos and expecting them to be Catholics and other things the Anglos didn't like. Since we had already read this before and had had a test on it, we knew that the Texas Revolution was coming up. At this point Doug McCallister, a kid I had never liked because he always tried to bully you until you called his bluff, had the brilliant idea that maybe we could re-enact the Texas Revolution, or at least the battle of the Alamo. Miss Gibbs didn't seem too sure that this was a good idea, but she said she would think about it.

That's how things stood for the next few days—with Miss Gibbs supposedly thinking over Doug's idea while we heard all sorts of rumors. We heard that the battle re-enactment was going to be held in Doug's father's place. We heard that Mr. McCallister's big barn was going to be the fort. We also heard that they were handing out roles already. Doug wanted to be Davy Crockett, and two of his buddies were going to be Jim Bowie and Travis. We, Mexicans, were going to be the Mexicans, of course, and, even if we won at the Alamo, we were going to get what was coming to us later.

I was trying to tune out all this hubbub and concentrate on baseball, but I got dragged into it, anyway. One afternoon, after school, I was with Pete and Osvaldo when we saw Lupita García, who was Pete's cousin, crying by the swings. She was sitting in a swing with her hands over her face, and we might have just ignored her, except that, standing by her was Alicia—I can't remember her last name—one of the best looking girls in the class, meaning one with the best developed breasts. We went over to where the girls were, trying to look concerned.

Alicia looked up at us with an expression of relief, as if now that the cavalry had arrived everything was going to be all right. "What's the matter with Lupita?" Pete asked her.

She spread out her hands, looking at all three of us. "I'm not sure. She just told me that Janey had been mean to her." Janey's father ran the bank in town, and she was the biggest pain in the butt, carrying on like she was royalty.

"What did Janey do to you? What did she say?" Pete asked his cousin, shaking her by the arm.

Lupita removed her hands from her face and, between sniffles, she told us how Janey had said that Mexicans had it coming to them. We had killed Davy Crockett; we were mean; we were stupid; we were dirty. When we had the fight at Doug's place, they were going to give us what we deserved. Then it was back to sniffling, but she seemed to feel a little better after telling somebody what was bothering her.

We told ourselves that Lupita was just being silly, like most girls, and we put her out of mind. Squabbles between girls did not concern us. But the next day Lupita was not at school. Nor the day after. After she had been gone two days, Pete and Osvaldo and I ran into her younger brother who was in the fourth grade, and Pete asked him what was wrong with his sister. He told us that she had stayed in bed the day before, saying that she had a stomach ache, and had done the same thing today.

"Maybe she got her period," said Osvaldo. "Girls get cramps when they have it." Pete and I looked embarrassed, but it went right past Lupita's kid brother.

"I don't know," the kid said, "but they're going to take her to the doctor if she doesn't get better."

Things went from bad to worse. First, Doug McCallister and his buddies picked a fight with some of us when we were going home on the bus, and the driver pulled off the road and threatened to beat us up if we didn't cut it out. Then he made Doug and his buddies sit up front and Pete and me and the rest in the back. The next day, when we were playing baseball, and I was at bat with Doug pitching, he threw a real close ball and hit me on the knuckles. My hand swelled up, and I couldn't play for days afterwards. Luckily, it was the left hand so I could still do things, and my father didn't find out. If there was something my father didn't want to do it was paying doctors' bills for sports-related injuries, as they say nowadays.

Then came the straw that broke the camel's back. I don't know how much out of things Miss Gibbs had to be to not realize the open hostility that had flared up between the Anglo and Mexican kids since she had started her "in-depth study" of the Texas Revolution. There had always been some tension, and Anglos didn't cross the line to be friends with Mexicans and vice versa, but while we were in suspense as to whether there would be a battle re-enactment, there was civil war brewing in the sixth grade. In the middle of this, on the next to the last week of school, Miss Gibbs came out with our final assignment for Texas history. Out of four or five major heroes of the Alamo—and she named Crockett, Bowie, Bonham, Travis and somebody else—each one of us was to select one and write a three--

page paper on him. We could give her our choice the next day.

That evening, while I sat at the kitchen table doing my homework and hiding my black and blue left hand—something I had also managed to do while eating, no mean feat—I chewed on my pencil, trying to decide on a hero to write about. All of a sudden I felt this wave of anger rising inside me. It confused me because always before if I was mad, I knew what I was mad at. Now it was different. I felt that I was starting to shake, and I wanted to start hitting things and throwing things around, but I knew I couldn't do that. If I did, my father would come in and start breaking my head. My mother came in the kitchen at that point and asked me if I was feeling sick. I must have looked a little strange. I said no, and she left. But I knew then why I was angry. I did not want to write a paper about any stupid hero. What did I care about the Battle of the Alamo? What did anybody care about something that happened over a hundred years ago? Stirring it all up only gave jerks like Doug McCallister and that Janey a chance to lord it over us, Mexicans. I wasn't going to write about any of those guys, and that was that.

But the next day I didn't have the guts to carry through with what I had decided the night before. When Miss Gibbs called on me to name my subject, I said "Jim Bowie," which was the first name that came into my head. Then she called on Osvaldo. She had called him "Waldo" ever since she found out that we called him "Valdo." Of course, in Spanish the "B" and the "V" come out pretty much alike, and he always spelled it "Baldo," but it didn't make any difference to him who called him what.

So there was Miss Gibbs, asking, "Waldo, what is *your* choice?"

"I'm gonna write about Gregorio Esparza."

Miss Gibbs was taken aback, but then she decided that Waldo must not have understood the assignment, and she explained again what it was all about. "That's all right, I understand," was Osvaldo's answer. "He—Gregorio Esparza—

was one of them." Miss Gibbs thought that maybe he still didn't understand and asked him if this *Gregoriuh* was a Mexican soldier. Osvaldo shook his head and said, "Nah, he was inside with the others. Got killed in there too." Miss Gibbs pulled a strategic retreat. She wasn't about to give in and let Osvaldo write about somebody that she had never heard of, so she said that she would have to look into it and let him know later.

After school Pete and I and others buzzed around Osvaldo, demanding that he tell us what he was up to. He had made up the name, hadn't he? Doug McCallister and his bunch went by at this time and made a few nasty gestures in our direction, but we ignored them. We kept asking Valdo where he had gotten the name that he had given Miss Gibbs. He kept putting us off, saying it was all in a history book. We knew he didn't even read the books he had to, and it certainly wasn't in *our* history book. Finally, Pete asked him if Gregorio Esparza had been related to him. "Yeah," Osvaldo answered him. "He was my . . . my father's grandfather." And that was all we got from him.

That night I was even madder than the night before. Why didn't I have a relative who had been a hero? And why didn't Miss Gibbs let Valdo write about Gregorio Esparza? The Gringos didn't know anything about us, Mexicans, about our history or anything. My grandfather had been a soldier, a colonel, I thought. I wished that I remembered my grandfather, but I had been only a year old when he died. If I had known him, he would have told me stories about his life in Mexico, and then I would have known about the heroes there. My father never talked about anything with me, except to scold me. Anyway, if Miss Gibbs didn't let Valdo write about his great-great grandfather, or whatever he was, then I would . . . I wouldn't . . . what? Here I stopped being furious, and the image of Lupita, staying home from school and confounding the doctors with her stomach aches, came to mind. I would stay home, too. I would not go to that school where all they did was put us down. I felt very proud of my decision and went to bed feeling pretty good.

The next day I had a stomach ache. I made a big production of running to the bathroom and staying there for a while until my mother knocked on the door and asked if there was anything wrong. I told her I had a runny stomach and stomach cramps, and that I thought I should stay home from school. She didn't say anything to that, and when I got out of the bathroom I had to go in the kitchen and repeat the whole thing for my father. He didn't look too convinced, but my mother touched my forehead and said that I felt hot and maybe I should stay home.

By that afternoon I was feeling pretty pleased with myself and having a great time reading comic books in bed when my father burst into the room. He had just realized that this was Friday afternoon, and his suspicious mind was telling him that I would make a recovery for the weekend. I am sure people could hear him shouting all the way to the road, which was a quarter of a mile away, and in Spanish, too, of course, so everybody could understand what he said. He hadn't whipped me in two or three years, but I could see his fingers twitching now around the belt, but still he didn't touch me. He said what I expected, that I was lazy, good-for-nothing, a loafer, and so on. Then he said some things I had not heard him say before.

He told me how hard he had worked to make sure all his kids got an education in the face of all the Gringos who didn't want Mexican kids in school. He said how, in spite of me being the youngest and likely to be the runt of the litter, I had turned out to be the smartest in school. Rufino, Jr., was a hard worker, and Roberto and Roel were slow but steady; but I actually seemed to have brains, and here I was, wasting them reading comic books and playing baseball. Didn't I know how hard it was for a Mexican to get ahead in this country? "Why didn't you go to school today?" he said. "I know you weren't sick."

I told him. I told him about the history class and about Doug and the other kids being nasty and about Miss Gibbs' assignment and how we had to write about Gringos who killed Mexicans but couldn't write about Mexicans. If I thought that my reasons would placate him, I was wrong.

He did not care about the Alamo and other ancient history. What did it matter who was or was not at the Alamo over a hundred years ago? What mattered was who had the jobs at Fort Sam Houston in San Antonio today. Did they hire Mexicans there? Not very many. What was important was, did you have property, did you have a good job? Where other Mexicans had been pushed out and run off, he had bought land, like his father before him, and worked it from sun up to sun down and improved it, so that even the Gringos respected him—well, maybe not respected him, they didn't respect Mexicans at all—but they gave him his due and didn't try to push him around. He had learned to take care of himself. Did I remember when the oil company had come to lease his land? No, maybe I didn't; that had been before I was born. Well, when the oil people had come, he didn't just sign where they told him to. He had gone to San Antonio and consulted with a lawyer there who told him how to get the best deal.

"That's what I mean," he added, dropping his voice and sounding very tired all of a sudden. "People survive because of force or brains. We don't have the force; we have to use brains. Some of us don't have much by way of brains, either, but you do. And you are wasting your brains, hanging out with *pachucos* and others who are never going to be anything. Do you want to spend the rest of your life sorting peanuts? If you don't, you had better go to school on Monday."

I spent the weekend working hard to make amends for my deceitfulness and didn't see any of the kids from school. A calf had gotten separated from his mother, and I spent all Sunday afternoon trying to coax him back across the fence. I managed to bring him back before nightfall, and, as I sat down to supper, I was feeling pretty virtuous, when my sister Yolanda, who had spent the day with us, noticed that I had a rash on my neck.

The following morning the rash was on my arms and

face and the rest of my body. Even my father told me to go back to bed while they decided if I had already had chicken pox and the measles. My mother was sure that I had. The doctor came in later and left some lotion for me to put on myself and said it looked like poison ivy. I had never known that we had any poison ivy around, but maybe it was down by the creek where I had been hunting for the calf.

The rash lasted for a couple of days, and it was pretty uncomfortable. I even had a temperature. I thought God was punishing me for pretending to be sick earlier, and at night I prayed to get well and promised never to fake being sick again.

All in all, I was gone from school for about a week, and when I got back, the class had already turned in their three-page papers on the heroes of the Alamo. I was excused from the assignment due to my illness, so I didn't have to write about Jim Bowie or whoever it was that I had selected. Osvaldo was not in school when I got back, but Pete told me that, although Valdo's paper on Gregorio Esparza had only been one page long, Miss Gibbs had given it a "B" and said that it was very good and even told the class some more about this Esparza guy that she had found out herself when she went up to the library in San Antonio.

Who the hell was Gregorio Esparza, anyway, I asked Pete, still feeling a little edgy from the itchiness. Not much of the report had sunk in Pete's brain, but he remembered that Gregorio Esparza had died fighting at the Alamo and that he had had his wife and children with him there. The family had survived, and the oldest of the children later told people what it had been like to be under attack.

"What do you know," said Pete, "it wasn't just Davy Crockett and all Gringos at the Alamo. There were some of us too. Valdo's grandfather."

Things quieted down as the school year wound to the end. Nobody talked anymore about staging the Battle of the Alamo in Doug's father's barn. I think Mr. Ewing had found out about it and put a lid on it. We went on the class trip to San Antonio and visited the Alamo. Osvaldo didn't go with us. We heard that his parents had pulled him out of school early because they were moving to California. I was sorry he had left because I had wanted to ask him some things about his famous ancestor, but I soon forgot about him with the excitement of the class trip and of going on to junior high.

We remembered Osvaldo, though, when we were going through the Alamo. I have never been real crazy about museums and ruins, and things were beginning to blur together after about an hour when Miss Gibbs pointed out a painting of a man in a torn shirt standing by a cannon on some kind of parapet. The painting represented Gregorio Esparza during the Battle of the Alamo, Miss Gibbs said. We looked at it for a few moments, and then Pete whispered in my ear: "He looks a little bit like Valdo, don't you think?"

✴

It was time that I got back on the road, or Rufus would be wondering what had happened to me. I left the Dairy Queen and drove across town. Just about a mile out of town, you turn left on to a county road, and then it's only about a fifteen-minute drive to the homeplace. The county road was in good shape with a fresh top dressing of caliche. I grinned as I drove on and saw a large sign tacked to two fence posts facing the road. It said, "Reelect Rufus Morales, County Commissioner." The old rascal sure got busy fixing roads when election time came around. It struck me all of a sudden that we had come a long way. Not just Rufus, but all of us, since the days when the Plantation Café in Poggendorf had had a sign that said, "We Do Not Serve Mexicans."

Some people had not changed much, though. Like Osvaldo. Just as I was leaving his truck stop, I finally asked him what I had not had a chance to ask him thirty years ago. As I was paying for the chewing gum, I asked him, "Was Gregorio Esparza really your ancestor?"

His eyes went blank as the windows of an empty house.

"Who? . . . Never heard of him."

I turned on my heel to leave. As I was reaching for the door, he raised his voice, higher than I had heard him speak till then, but just loud enough so I could hear him. "I made it up," he said.

I stopped, and before I could ask him why, he added, "I got tired of that kid that was always crying, that girl who said the Anglo girl was picking on her. Lupita. What happened to her? Did she stay in school?"

I could not remember what had happened to Lupita. All I remembered was that I did not remember her after the sixth grade. "No," I answered him. "I don't think that she stayed in school."

"That's too bad." He went back to the table with the truck driver and his passenger, and I left.

As I got out to open the gate to the ranch, I was wondering where Osvaldo had heard of Gregorio Esparza. He was not in the history books that we had read. Even Miss Gibbs didn't know about him. Then it struck me that Valdo had already been to the Alamo before us. I could not help laughing and shaking my head at the thought. Rufus and his road repairs. Osvaldo and his famous ancestor. My father would have been pleased.